Dance With the Devil

Blake Detective Series, Volume 1

Jon Mason

Published by Jon Mason Books, 2023.

This is a work of fiction. Similarities to real people, places, or events are entirely coincidental.

DANCE WITH THE DEVIL

First edition. June 12, 2023.

Copyright © 2023 Jon Mason.

ISBN: 978-1916757097

Written by Jon Mason.

To my mother who instilled in me a love of literature

Dance with The Devil

Jon Mason

A faint groan escaped from the tightly bound roll of carpet. Vince Cabot smiled at the protest and kicked it again for good measure. He bent forwards. Almost whispering. 'Celeste was fifteen. How long had you been screwing her? I did warn you what would happen if you ever came back. Now, I'm going to do the people of this county a favour. I hope you enjoyed your nineteenth birthday, Patrick. There won't be another.'

Cabot glanced up at the night sky and pulled his coat tighter. The rain had stopped. Just a smattering of stars visible. His daughter's bedroom light muted by the curtains. Patrick Kemp had seduced his last underage girl.

Carpet safely in the back of his van Patrick began his final journey.

Kemp was the bane of the county. His father, Quincey, owner of several fairground attractions. Quincey was ok, as honest as the day was long. On the other hand, Patrick was just like the Barkers of bygone days. Young. Rugged good looks. A ready smile. And, a dangerous almost hypnotic and dangerous way with the girls. Quincey had given up on him. He tried his best but Patrick answered to no man. Now, he would answer to gravity.

Patrick Kemp was still spinning when the scream died. Thirty feet above at the quarry's edge Vince Cabot folded the carpet pushing it into his van, it would be ideal for the office above his new shop. A red stain on a dark red carpet? Disinfectant would take care of that.

Like everyone else in the district he was interviewed by the police. Yes, he had seen Patrick Kemp two days before his father reported him missing. He was pragmatic. After he found out that Kemp had had sex with his daughter, he warned him – if he came anywhere near the house again he would get a clout and, passed the message on to his father. When Kemp turned up on his land and said he wanted to marry his daughter? ... There was more chance of there being a God.

Constable William Chapman made the initial enquiries. 'Bill, you're a copper. You've got two daughters. Apart from Celeste only being fifteen would you want that little bastard as a son-in-law? No? Look, I gave the little turd a clout. Sent him on his way. The last time I saw him he was alive.' His wife, Vanda, couldn't help. Neither could Celeste. His son, Walter, away at university.

The police, with Vince's permission, searched the farmhouse and outbuildings. No trace. They came back with a search warrant and emptied the barn – his furniture store – still nothing. Three prison sentences for violence in his twenties. He was still a suspect.

The dark red carpet, bought for ten shillings in an auction, looked well in the office. Office? To be honest it had been a shit-tip. Full of useless crap. The detritus went to the tip. Buckets of hot water, disinfectant, sugar soap and elbow grease did the rest. *Unfortunately,* the disinfectant *fell* off the table. He stood and watched as the gurgles soaked the carpet. Shame. The smell would last for months.

The cellar was cavernous, stretching way beyond the rear of the property. Probably completely under the service road. A large double hatch at the rear of the shop, an ideal store room. Get some of the furniture out of his barn. However, before the concrete could be delivered the floor had to be levelled. That wasn't going to happen by itself.

Detective Inspector Cosmo Trevithick, report in hand, looked across his desk at the young detective constable. 'Blake, you came here straight from Bishopgarth following your initial CID course six months ago. With virtually no experience your crystal ball is telling you the Co-op in Station Road is going to get screwed this coming Friday? You're serious?'

'Quite possibly, sir. There or thereabouts. That's the average, one hundred and twenty-seven days.'

'I can read, Blake, thank you,' the sarcasm dripping from his tongue. 'It goes with the job.' The detective inspector thought rapidly, *if he's right and I do nothing I'll look a pillock. If he's wrong, well, that's his affair. Upstairs.* 'I can't cover the overtime for this. I'll see the superintendent, see what he thinks. But, don't hold your breath. Now, go do some police work.'

Superintendent Bulstrode did not suffer fools and Trevithick was not. He sat back in his chair and glared. 'You're giving credence to this, Trevithick?' He wafted the report. 'There's no independent information?'

'The figures are right, sir. And, no, there's just Blake's calculation.'

The superintendent removed a blue manilla folder from his filing cabinet. 'Douglas Blake. Married with a five year old son. Engineer. Three years police service pre-WW2. Ex-RAF. Passed his promotion exams – good mark. Good mark on CID course.' He replaced the folder and picked up the phone. 'Bulstrode. Is Blake still in the building, sergeant? ... He is? Send him up.'

'What gave you the idea, Blake?'

'I was looking through the index cards, sir. The Co-op seemed to be very popular and the crimes are still undetected. Possibly regular visitors, so I worked out the figures.'

'Is the MO the same?'

'Varies sir. Loading bay. Rear window. Side door.'

'Which days of the week?'

'Payday to Saturday, sir.'

'How many others have you told?'

'Other than Sergeant Roberts, no-one, sir.'

'Keep it that way. I'm not paying overtime. Thursday, Friday, and Saturday you will work 10-6 nights. Go and speak with the manager. Tell him that we have some non-specific information about a break-in. Under no circumstances will you reveal to anyone your calculations. If you are correct, which I doubt very much, we would have the world and his wife demanding protection on what could be a fluke. Explain, with his permission, you will spend those nights on the premises. He is to tell no-one. Your visit today is purely crime prevention. You will require a key which you will retain for those three nights.

Inspector, speak with the shift inspector for those nights. Again, no mention of those calculations. Just a watching brief on the Co-op. No hanging about in the area. Extra patrols could draw unwarranted attention.'

On the second day Vince Cabot's pick struck something massive. Hard as the Devil's forehead. Full width of the cellar. Eighteen inches high curving away. The bricks narrow and very old. One of his barns was 17th century with similar sized bricks. Covered by over a foot of compacted soil. An hour later he returned with a torch, hurricane lamp, matches, fuel and his tool box. Whoever had built it had made a damn good job. It took ten minutes to knock the first brick through into what lay beneath. Twenty minutes later a lighted piece of paper dropped into the void showed what appeared to be a tunnel, four feet across and bone dry. At least it wasn't a sewer.

He wasn't an excitable man but there were exceptions. An hour later. Twenty bricks stacked to one side he lay on the floor poked his head through the hole and shone his torch right and left. A tunnel it was. Tall enough to stand in. Passable as far as he could see. There were no rodent tracks. Rats? He hated rats. Fifty yards to the right the tunnel curved to the left. Ten yards to the right a partial collapse. No problem, there was a market for old bricks. Left was different. An uphill gradient. He lowered himself and paced one hundred and ninety seven steps. A side tunnel to the left ended in a low studded-door. Solid and locked. 'Where the hell does this lead?' he muttered to himself. Torch off, the stygian darkness closed in. Through the keyhole there was a lightness. Not enough to see by but it was lighter. It had to be a room, but where? Once again in the main tunnel he managed another eighty-three steps before coming to a partial roof collapse. It looked as if a good sneeze would bring the lot down.

The sign read. *One ring for attention. Please!* He rang twice.

'Can I ... Oh hello Vince. Come to have a look round the museum?'

'Noreen,' he acknowledged. 'Vanda was only saying the other day we hadn't seen you. You're working here?'

'Only part-time. I'll drop her a line. Now what can we do for you?'

He took the brick from his carrier-bag. 'Apart from being told it's old, Noreen, is there anyone here who might be able to tell me about it?'

David Thomas, post graduate archaeology student studying for his PhD, took the brick turning it over in his hands several times. 'Sorry,' he looked up with a guilty smile and offered his hand. 'My manners, David, David Thomas,' he said.

'Vince Cabot,' he replied. They shook hands.

'Could I ask where you got it from?'

'I've got a farm out towards Doncaster. I rent the land out. This,' he indicated the brick. 'I dug up some months ago and put it in the barn, that's 17th century. It's similar. But there aren't any missing that I can see.'

'Ok.' David Thomas looked again. *This hasn't been buried, there's only dirt on one edge. Other than that, apart from mortar, it's clean. Still, nothing to do with me.* 'We're in the way here, Vince. Come into the office.'

'Well, it's too small to be Roman. Lagentium was the legion at Castleford and it would have had their stamp on the edge.' He ferreted round in a drawer and found a ruler measuring the brick carefully. 'It's nine inches long, four and a half wide and two inches and a quarter thick. That puts it between 1571 when a charter specified that all bricks should be 9 x 4.5 x 2.25 inches and the 18th century act of parliament which specified they must be 8.5 x 4 x 2.5 inches. More than that I can't say. But it's a nice find.'

'Thanks. So that makes it in the same time scale as my barn, always assuming the date I was given was correct.'

'Looks like it. And this was the only one?'

'Yes.'

'Er, would it be possible to come and have a look round, take some measurements.'

'Not a problem.'

It was something of a rarity but Bulstrode was smiling. The atmosphere upbeat. DI Trevithick, Inspector Groves, DS Roberts and DC Blake were facing him across his desk.

'What were you doing back there, Blake. You'd had three days, why go back for a fourth and in *your own time*?' He added, stressing the last three words.

'I still had the key, sir. I was going to return it this morning. But ... I thought I'd give it until 2am. I was just on the point of leaving when I heard the skylight going through.'

'Excellent! Groves?'

'Blake's phone call came as a bit of a surprise. Simpkins was half nights and just about to leave when the call came through. So, in all, with meal change overs and including supervision we had seven, plus a double-manned traffic car. We surrounded the building. The one on the roof jumped and broke an ankle. He's in the infirmary with a uniform to keep him company. Blake had the other two cuffed. It was over in ten minutes.'

'Excellent. Interviews?' He looked at Blake.

'Singing like canaries sir,' he replied. 'One of them is Charlie Pilbeam, the manager's brother. The manager is on his way in. They're all blaming each other. Couldn't be better.'

'How many offences so far?'

'Eight, sir. Five at the Co-op, two local working men's clubs and one so far in Dewsbury.'

'Perfect. Blake, have you had anything to eat?'

'I managed to grab a sandwich when the butchers opened.'

'Good. Trevithick, the time that Blake has worked since 2am, put an extra day onto his next weekend off.' Both acknowledged. 'Dismissed.'

'He didn't give you the time back between ten and two?'

Blake shook his head. 'No sarge.'

DS Roberts chuckled. 'You know, he's as tight as a duck's arse and they're water tight. One thing though, young Charlie Pilbeam has admitted they originally intended to do the place on the Saturday. So well done. Go get some sleep. You'll be shown as arresting officer and OIC. Come back on for four. Get your statement out of the way. Once the file's gone in you can concentrate on the job in hand.'

'Ok, sarge. But it will only work for business premises that have been hit several times. The more the better. There's no guarantee.'

He nodded. 'I appreciate that, Blake. Remember, you've got Bulstrode well and truly fired-up so don't waste it. This success won't do you any harm. And don't spread it around why you're collating the details.'

Utilising fallen bricks he built a couple of steps. It took five days to clear the fallen bricks and stack them in the cellar. He bought a 7lb ball of sisal string – over 440 yards in length and measured the tunnels.

To the right there had been a total collapse after seventy yards. To the left, the main tunnel was dead straight for two hundred and eighty-three yards. Ten yards further another collapse. That was as far as he could get.

Adjacent and to the right there had been an opening of some description, probably a staircase which had been bricked-up leaving the face of the bottom step exposed. Again, bricks of the same dimensions. How far underground he was or what lay above he had no idea, although the direction took him towards the city centre.

The door at the end of the side-tunnel was forty-one yards from the main tunnel. Using his father's prismatic compass, the direction of the main tunnel was 283 degrees magnetic. Just what was up top? If he was right?

Slowly a plan began to form. He needed maps. Old maps.

Celeste was developing an addiction to pleasure. She told virgin David Thomas she was seventeen prior to having sex the first time on an 18th century Loo table at the back of her father's barn. The blastocyte implanted in the wall of her uterus five days later. Implantation complete on the ninth day – the day they had unprotected sex for the seventh time. For the purposes of procreation the last six occasions had been superfluous. The following day, whilst her mother was visiting her grandma at home, David helped to keep her bed warm for a couple of hours.

'Sorry, Celeste,' he said as he was leaving. 'They're asking questions at work about the time I spend here. Plus, I've got an assignment to get finished. I can't get here so often.'

'What?' she pouted. 'Now you had your leg over you're dumping me?'

'No, far from it. I just can't get here as often.'

'Oh, shame,' she draped her arms round his neck and kissed him. 'What if I'm pregnant?'

His face paled. 'You're pregnant?'

'Not that I know of, David. But what if I am. I am a bit young.'

'I suppose seventeen is a bit young. If you were.'

Her eyes full of mischief, she grinned. 'I'm only fifteen,' she whispered in his ear.

'What? You said you were seventeen.'

She grinned again. 'Did I say that? But you didn't use a johnny, did you? I might be. You never know. But it was nice and *you* enjoyed it. And, if I were, well ... Dad would not be pleased.'

Chris Bellamy had one conviction for shop-lifting five years ago as a juvenile. He was placed on probation for 12 months. He had none for breaking into premises. He was good. As instructed he had delivered the maps in a sack. All of them. Every single map he could find in the reference section of the library and pocketed the £25 offered by Vince, guaranteeing silence. It was healthier that way.

Of all the faults that Vince Cabot had, the lack of a sense of humour was not included. He chuckled to himself as he turned them over, one-by-one. There were 173 in total. The 152nd gave him the information that might provide the answer. The rest could wait. They might be useful. No. 152 the town centre. Dated 1593. Painted on vellum in what had been bright colours; it was a work of art and relevant. The road outside was now called Water Lane, then, Water Hill. Terminating in the Bull Ring and still named as such although the cattle market was now a quarter of a mile away. To the left the parish church of All Souls. All roads led to the Bull Ring: Northgate, Westgate, Southgate, and Water Hill. Shop door locked. A quick check of the compass – 283 degrees magnetic. It was time to visit the bank.

An hour later he shook hands with Bryson Donaldson, Manager of the Northern General Bank. 'Thanks for everything,' he said, displaying the key to his safe deposit box. 'It's perfect.'

'You won't regret it, Mr Cabot. We will see you in due course.'

Vince Cabot smiled and turned away raising his right hand in acknowledgement. Over the roof of the Garden Restaurant the clock tower of All Souls beckoned.

Rumours had come his way that his friend, Archdeacon Desmond Tempest, had his hand in the till to settle his gambling debt with a local bookie. He had nowhere near enough. The church was calling.

'Well, well, well, what is a heathen like Vince Cabot doing in a sacred place like All Souls?'

Cabot smiled. 'Good morning, Desmond. You're in fine form this morning. I've come to see you.'

'What?' the look of amazement broken by a broad smile. 'You've come to repent?' he said. The scenario playing out along well-established lines. 'You're seeking divine forgiveness?'

'Now Desmond, how likely is that?'

'Sadly,' he sighed. 'Most unlikely. Now, what can I do for you, Vince?'

'The first recording of a church on this site was during the reign of Stephen and Matilda. Consecrated in 1142. It burnt down and was rebuilt 1246 – that's the reign of Henry III. In 1294 Edward I granted the town a Market Charter. The town expanded and the money rolled in. During the reign of Charles II, in 1671, it was rebuilt after yet another fire. Sounds like a combination of clerics with too much communion wine and too many lit candles.'

The Archdeacon ignored the barb. 'I'll say one thing, Vince, you know your history. But where is this tale going?'

'I deal in antiques, Desmond. It's my job to know history. From research that I've done it appears that some of the damaged church furniture, including the Roodscreen, is in your cellar.'

'Cellar?' iterated the Archdeacon. 'I've never been in the cellar. I wouldn't know.'

'Well, it appears that you have. I've recently helped other churches by taking some of their redundant furniture off their hands ...'

The Archdeacon, his mind whirring, full of the possibilities, interrupted. 'And you want to relieve All Souls of theirs?'

'Not exactly. Pre 20th century ecclesiastical furniture is selling very well in the United States through the auction houses. I can do the same for you.'

'You mean buy for a pittance and make a fortune for yourself?'

'Certainly not. I might not believe in your God but I do not cheat people. For 20% of the hammer price I will make all the arrangements and get it to the right place. You just pay the auction house commissions and local taxes. All bone fide.' *And, you owe some bad people a lot of money.*

'You're serious?'

'Money is no joking matter, Desmond. Ring Father Casey at English Martyrs or Reverend Wilkins at St. Catherine's. I've done the same for them. Give them a call, it can't hurt.'

He turned to leave. 'Don't take too long, Desmond. I have space booked on a freighter leaving for the States in four weeks.' *Gus Roberts will wait a little longer,* he thought, *but there is a limit before he takes his pound of flesh.* 'There won't be another until next March. Contact me at home or I'll call in when I'm passing.' Business was good and he had space booked on freighters heading for the American auction houses every two months. There was nothing wrong in instilling a little fear of loss.

The atmosphere in the Superintendent's office was oppressive. Superintendent Bulstrode looked at the two sheets of paper side-by-side on his desk. 'This is the full list, Blake?' He indicated the sheet on his left.

'Yes sir, all commercial, all undetected,' he replied. 'I've checked for the last five years.'

'But some of these are on the High Street.' He indicated the second sheet. 'Explain this to me again. I don't like the way you put it.'

'From left to right sir: Date of recording: Crime number and beat: Officer taking the complaint and shift: The shift that was working during the times listed on the crime complaint.'

'And your figures show that shift two were working during 74% of the times when these crimes were committed.'

'Yes, sir. I wasn't looking for that but I noticed the regularity and checked the duty rosters. It came as a shock.'

Bulstrode paused. 'You've got plenty of work to do, Blake?'

'Yes, sir,' he turned and left the office.

'It's a pretty kettle of fish Trevithick, make no mistake. I take it no-one else is aware of these figures?'

'No-one, sir. And, I trust Blake to keep his mouth shut.'

'So do I. Right, get the No2 books out of store. Division if necessary.'

'Already done, sir. And the crime files. Blake took it on himself.'

'Did he now?' Bulstrode looked at the detective inspector and smiled. 'Is he after your job?'

'One of these days, sir, he might have it. I've shown him duty elsewhere for two days and given permission for him to work from home. There's nowhere in the station private enough to do the analysis he has to do.'

Very well, Trevithick. Keep me appraised.'

Vanda Cabot smiled at Celeste's news. 'You silly girl. We thought you'd learned your lesson after Patrick. Who is it, David?'

Celeste nodded. 'I didn't get pregnant with Patrick.'

'And you thought you wouldn't again and didn't use anything? Celeste, you should know better than that. And you told him you were seventeen?'

Celeste nodded and smiled. 'He is nice.'

Vanda raised her eyebrows and smiled. 'I'm glad you think so, you're probably carrying his child. There's no wonder he was always here. It wasn't just a one-off, was it.'

'No.'

'Well, you can't turn the clock back. As for what your father will say.'

The following evening Vince, Vanda, Celeste, and David sat in the lounge. 'So, David, now you know. You both like each other but do you like each other enough? Celeste will be sixteen in seven weeks. She's probably carrying your child and, whether you thought that she was seventeen or not you didn't use a condom. You must have realised the possibilities that this could happen, or didn't you care?'

'I didn't think. It just happened.'

'It wasn't your brain that was doing the thinking, was it?' said Vanda. 'Celeste told you she was seventeen and came on to you. And don't look at me like that, young lady,' she continued as Celeste scowled at her. 'David is not Patrick. He came out here from the museum because of a brick your father had discovered not to get involved with you. You must accept some of the responsibility.'

'The question is, Celeste, it's only been a few weeks but do you want David in your life or, bring the baby up by yourself? Do you want to see him again?' He held his hand up before Celeste could answer. 'The same applies to you David. Was Celeste just a quick thrill, or, do you want her and the baby, if she's pregnant, in your life?' he glanced at his wife. 'Come on Vanda we'll go to the Shepherds for an hour whilst these two talk it through.'

'You were easy on him, Vince,' said Vanda as they left the farm. 'Not like you were with Patrick.'

'Different animal, love,' he smiled at himself in the rear-view mirror.

'And you were saving the threat of a possible prison sentence for under age sex, and a paternity order from the magistrate's court just in case?'

'You know me so well. Plus, I wanted them to talk it through without any threats. What's the betting that she has him in her bed well before we get to the pub ... There's an old saying that sex can pull a man further than dynamite can blow him. He's a studious young man and doesn't appear to have many close friends. From what I've heard, none of them are female. I'll bet Celeste was his first.'

'His last?'

The two days became four. Douglas Blake presented his analysis to Detective Inspector Trevithick and Superintendent Bulstrode. 'So, Blake, either Frobisher, Martin or Gledhill were working the beats concerned at the relevant times with the other two on adjoining beats. The total value of the property reported stolen over the five years is £22,457 and a few pence.'

'That's correct, sir. Crime reports for the premises on the list are being made in rotation. However, you'll see there is no clear target. Nothing stands out. It's either three or four breaks.'

Bulstrode nodded. 'Gledhill is next. Ten days. When shift two are working nights?'

'Yes, sir ... With respect, can I make a suggestion?'

'Go ahead.'

'Taking the pragmatic approach. The crimes have been recorded. Nothing can change that. Nothing stands out as a probable target. Would it be possible to split them? Transfer, for example, Gledhill. Spread the group.'

'Possibly. Where do you suggest?'

'Far end of the county, sir. Uppermill, Doncaster or Rotherham divisions. Somewhere they would find it difficult to get back here. None of them have their own transport."

'No clear target?'

'No, sir.'

Bulstrode paused, checked the list again and smiled. 'Blake, suppose they were given a fright and decided to commit one last crime, which of the list might you pick? There are twenty-seven premises?'

'One of the three chemists, sir.'

'Pick one.'

'Dock Street is the largest. Dresden Road has the largest total.'

Bulstrode nodded. 'Very well. Take Dresden Road. The same rules as last time. Next Tuesday speak with the chemist in confidence. No specific information etc. Need to borrow a key for the weekend, Friday to Monday. Not a word to anyone. Understood?'

'Yes, sir.'

'Dismissed.'

The door closed behind Blake. 'Trevithick, I'll authorise it. One DC from Batley and one from Hecton. Interview independently. Utmost secrecy. One in each of the other two chemists. Same rules. Not a word to anyone.'

A week of clearing the fallen bricks and no message from the archdeacon Vince Cabot was almost knocked down in the rush as the choirboys left. 'Steady on boys,' he laughed. 'You'll have me over. Is the Archdeacon about?'

'He's in the sacristy, sir,' said one.

'He's punishing Michael for laughing at him,' said another.

'For what?' said Cabot as the boys ran off. He shrugged his shoulders and entered the church. His attention drawn to the sound of a boy crying and a raised voice coming from the sacristy.

He opened the door and froze. The archdeacon, back to the door, was smacking a young lad around the head with both hands. 'I'll beat the Devil out of you Michael Nelson. I'll teach you to mock me.'

He stepped forward seizing the archdeacon's wrist. 'What the hell are you playing at Desmond?' he said. 'He's only a child.'

The flushed archdeacon glared at Cabot. 'Not your business, Vince,' he said. 'Now let go.'

'When a grown man beats a defenceless child I make it my business.' He let go and turned to the boy. 'Are you all right, son?' he said.

Michael Nelson wiped his eyes with the back of his hand and nodded.

'Right, off you go and whatever it was, don't do it again. All right?'

The boy departed. 'Right, Desmond, let's say no more and have a look in your cellar.'

The vaulted room was huge, most of it stuffed with furniture. 'Good God, Desmond, you've enough stuff here for a couple of trailers. More than enough to pay Gus Roberts off.'

'I'll thank you not to blaspheme. And what has Gus Roberts got to do with anything?'

'I'm not stupid, Desmond. Not very subtle, are you? Just how much do you owe him?'

'None of your business.'

'Well, I'll tell you this for nothing. He's getting anxious. So, what's it to be?'

Martin and Lavinia Thomas were not happy.

'I'm sorry my son's got your daughter into trouble, Mr Cabot,' said Martin Thomas, 'but to throw his life away because of it I find unacceptable. It will ruin his chances of ever making something of himself.'

'That's your final word. If David and Celeste marry you don't want to know and won't support them?'

Lavinia Thomas was annoyed. 'Certainly not.'

'That's what they call blackmail. My way or the highway.'

'Very crude, but yes. Celeste is far too young and David has minimal experience.'

Vanda laughed. 'I think you'll find that David has more experience than you thought.'

These people, Lavinia thought. 'I wasn't meaning that.'

'I'm sure you weren't,' said Vanda.

'Do I get the chance to speak? It is my life that you're discussing.'

'David, please.'

'Mother. You might not like it but I have my degree. The PhD was a bonus. I can always finish later and I can get a job in teaching. If that's what you intend, then so be it.'

'Just a second,' interjected Vince as Martin Thomas was about to speak. He gave Vanda a questioning look. She nodded. 'David. Celeste, your mother and I have discussed the situation and this is what we are prepared to do. We will support you financially. David can stay here and we will renovate the old cottage. It's not bad, just needs a spruce-up. We'll show you round tomorrow. You can live there rent free. In due course, if David wants, he can learn about my business. He's an archaeologist. I deal in antique furniture. He's half way there.'

'And another thing,' said Vanda. 'Once married you will be his wife. And that is not just about having babies. You will have to learn to cook etc. What's it to be?'

David and Celeste grinned at each other. 'What have we got to lose, Celeste. Shall we?' She nodded.

'Thank you,' said David, 'That's very kind. We accept.'

Douglas Blake was beginning to doze when he heard the rear door splinter. A quick phone call and he was standing behind the door connecting the store room with the dispensary. As soon as he heard items being moved he pounced. Peter Gledhill started as he cleared his throat.

'What? Oh it's you, Douglas. I was just checking the rear of the property and found the door insecure.'

'That's strange, Peter, two minutes before you jemmied it, it was sound. You're nicked.'

'What are you talking about. I was checking the property.'

'Of course you were. Checking to make sure it was safe to screw the place. We weren't sure which one of you it would be. Now I know.' He put his hand on Gledhill's shoulder. 'I know you know the caution. But, you're not obliged to say anything ...'

First to arrive was DS Roberts. 'Well done, Douglas. We're picking the other two up now. Peter Gledhill. Couldn't resist one last job, could you. Well, as an ex-copper your next one will be fighting the villains off in prison.

'Well,' Superintendent Bulstrode was smiling. 'I was hoping that you would be wrong, Blake. Three bent coppers are not good. It's going to look worse when the Press get their teeth into it. But at least we can be seen tidying up our own mess. Already they're coughing and passing the buck. Blake, I think you will understand when I say I want to keep you out of the limelight.'

'Yes sir. I do.'

'Good. Trust me. You will still get the credit. All I want from you is a simple statement of arrest. Inspector Trevithick will be responsible for explaining about the information.

The four of them stood and looked at the cottage.

'It will take some elbow grease but it's all right.'

Celeste was unimpressed. 'But all the plaster's falling down,' she said.

'That's superficial, Celeste. You'll see.'

With just cause most people were frightened of him. The man walking in his direction you could only treat in one fashion – with kid gloves.

Alistair McGreevy, member of one of Glasgow's notorious razor gangs pulled the chair out and sat. He was due to be released in six weeks having served ten years for robbery with violence.

'Vince.' The Scots accent thick enough to saw boards.

'Hello Alistair,; he said. Small talk was not something Alistair McGreevy was good at. 'I'm planning a welcome home party for you in four weeks,'

Four? I dinna get out for another six.'

'In four weeks, you've got a perfect alibi.'

His eyes narrowed. 'What's your offer?'

'Thirty percent.'

'Fifty.'

'Split the difference?'

'Done. What do you want?'

'I'm planning some exotic desserts, gelly always goes down well.'

'That all?'

'I can arrange everything else. I just need a specialist.'

'You know my brief?'

'Yes.'

'I want him here as soon as possible. He'll be in touch. Any idea of the presents?'

'No. There's a lot to unwrap.'

'Anything else?'

'Not that I can think of.'

'You pay the specialist.'

'Of course.'

'Your friend the archdeacon. I hear you caught him clattering a young lad.'

'Yep, the kid was being cheeky. I stepped in.'

'Good. You know he was caught raping a choirboy?'

This was troubling. What adults did was up to them but children. That was different. 'No, I didn't.'

'Threatened the boy with Hellfire if he told. The boy's father walked in. Stupid bastard didn't bar the door. The police are useless so he told Ben, my cousin. Rather than float his miserable corpse down the Clyde he was advised south of the border would be healthier.

Leave something from the kitty left where it might be found. Something of sufficient interest to rouse Gus Roberts.'

'You don't miss much, Alistair.'

'Vince, I don't miss anything. Any further through my brief.' He stood.

The visit was over.

'There's nothing else suitable, Blake?'

Douglas Blake looked at the superintendent's expression and smiled. 'Sorry, sir. There are plenty with two or even three but spread out over the five years. Nothing I would care to put money on.'

'Very well. Keep a daily eye on the crime figures. Let me know should anything come to mind.'

A week to go to the wedding. David Thomas was sharing Celeste's bed and had begun his education into the world of antiquities. Between them he and Vince were transporting truckloads of artifacts to Vince's barn.

An extra bonus for Vince. A massive ancient key found trodden into the earthen floor close to the door. He would try the lock from the opposite side..

Vince gave David the job of historical research

Archdeacon Tempest's eyes widened as he read the document:

I, Desmond Tempest, Archdeacon of All Souls, do hereby grant permission for Vince Cabot to remove the redundant furniture and other articles from the church cellar. He has my authority to dispose of the said articles and tranship to the United States of America for sale by public auction for a consideration of 20% of the hammer price.

The remainder, less the seller's commission and taxes, to be returned to the church.

Signed

'Vince, I can't sign this,' he handed the document back.

'Well, I can't do what we agreed without an authority can I? I'd be wide open to allegations of stealing church property. Come on Desmond there's nothing contentious. You need this. Just sign it. Father Casey and the Reverend Wilkins signed the same document. You stand to make a lot more money than they did. The sooner we start the sooner you get Gus off your back.'

He signed.

Malcolm 'Twine' Baler and Peter Smith 'Smithy' had always been rivals. Both wanted to be the Boss. When they became step-brothers it didn't get any better. Twine's father, Jack, was quick to anger and fast with his fists. Doreen tried to keep the peace but it was a lost cause. Both were regularly in trouble and had served terms in Borstals. Any excuse for a fight.

Frank Nevison was a direct descendent of John 'Swift Nick' Nevison, the 17th century gentleman Highwayman, or so he claimed. Unlike Swift Nick he didn't carry a brace of Peter Meeson flintlock pistols. Instead, beneath the bar of The Barge, always within reach was a well-used hickory pickaxe shaft. The sawn-off shotgun hadn't seen the light of day for a long time. He called across the bar and laughed. 'Vince, I got some fresh milk for those two six year olds.'

Twine looked over his shoulder. 'Fuck off!'

Vince Cabot smiled and shook his head. 'Twine, sit down. Shake hands with Smithy.'

'Shake hands with this piece of shit, Vince? You must be joking.'

'Twine, sit-down.'

With a bad grace Twine sat.

A large hand grabbed him by the back of his shirt collar and twisted, hoisting the struggling Twine to his feet gasping for breath. 'Ever speak to me like that again or I'll forget your father's a friend. Blink if you understand.'

He blinked as he fought to get his breath back and rubbed his throat.

'Sorry.'

'That's better. Now, be a good little boy and do as Vince says. Shake hands. Think before you open your mouth in future.'

'Act like that again I won't be as gentle,' said Vince. 'Right, you two claim to have some handy lads.'

'We have,' said Smithy. Twine nodded.

'Right, this is what you're going to do.'

Douglas Blake stared at his wife. 'Dorothy, are you sure it was them?'

'Positive. Twine and Smithy coming out of The Crown, together with their girlfriends, laughing. Like old friends.'

'But they hate each other.'

'Not from what I saw they don't.'

'Could you hear what was said?'

She frowned and smiled. 'Do I get paid overtime for this?'

He put his hands on her hips and smiled. 'Well?'

She reciprocated. 'Oh, all right. Twine said something about a nice little earner and more to come. They all laughed,' she scowled at him. 'I didn't hear anything else. Now, if you want your dinner on time, out of my kitchen.

11am. Celeste Cabot left the church of All souls as Celeste Thomas. There were two dozen guests. Martin Thomas sat at the back of the nave. Lavinia Thomas refused to attend her son's wedding.

'Baler and Smith friends?'

'So it appears, sir. If they get together it could spell trouble.'

'There's no could, Blake ... Those two in harness ... And your wife didn't hear anything else?'

'No sir. She was walking in the opposite direction.'

Change of plan. The furniture had been removed from the Church cellars and was now safely in his second barn. The timber to build the packing cases would be delivered in three days. What McGreevy had told him about Desmond's predilection for young boys was troubling.

He smiled to himself. The plan would work. Vanda had warned him. "Whatever you're planning, Vince, keep the children out of it. And that includes David. He might be a clever lad but he'll never be up for your antics.' There was no hiding anything from her. She knew him too well, and, she was right.

It only took a few hours to remove the bricks and expose the staircase. He had been concerned that it might have been back-filled. It wasn't. Fifteen steps to a concrete floor. If his measurements were right, the floor of the Northern General Bank safe deposit. The bricks stacked in the side-tunnel adjacent to the church door.

Next, forget about selling the bricks from the tunnel. Now it had been weakened it was just a matter of brute force with a sledgehammer. Demolish the rest and stack all the fallen bricks as a foundation to his own cellar extension.

It was a sombre crowd standing at the water's edge. 'What do you think, Douglas?' PC Graeme Valentine grimaced. 'Patrick Kemp?'

Douglas Blake snorted a laugh. 'Difficult to tell without a face. Apart from it's similar. One thing that is strange though. Look at the way he's lying. He's what.' He took his tape measure from the small tin in his pocket. 'Four feet three inches from the quarry face and almost parallel. Almost as if he'd rolled off the top. If he'd jumped or been pushed or thrown he'd have been further out and in a heap. He looks as if he landed flat on his face.'

'At least he wouldn't have suffered.'

'Perhaps. Come on Graeme, let's get him out. Let the pathologist take a look. Where's the man who spotted the body?'

Photographs taken, the body placed on a stretcher and winched to the top of the quarry courtesy of the fire brigade.

Patrick Wilson, his black Labrador back on its leash, looked sick. 'I've never seen a dead person before.'

'It can be disconcerting Mr Wilson, especially one like this …I shall require a statement either today or tomorrow. What time would be best?'

'7pm, officer.'

'That's fine. And you will be required to give evidence at the inquest.'

'Do I have to?'

Douglas Blake laughed. 'Fraid so. The coroner will want to speak to you. Until this evening.'

DI Trevithick put the sudden death report on his desk. 'You've got the clothing, Blake?'

'Yes sir. From the description on the Misper the clothing matches. But he's not in a fit state for viewing.'

Trevithick nodded. 'As soon as the photos arrive, I want to see them.'

'Yes sir.'

'That quarry's what, eight or ten miles from Vince Cabot's place?'

'It is.'

'Take the Misper. Irrespective of whether you get a positive id find Cabot and have another go at him. Plus, all the others who were interviewed. I know it's a month old and any trail will be cold but you never know. When's the PM?'

'10.00am tomorrow sir.'

Vince Cabot switched his torch off. Silence and darkness impenetrable. 'Well Bill, what do you think?' He turned the torch back on.

Bill Nolan, Alistair McGreevy's turn-to for exotic desserts smiled. He had driven past the bank on several occasion wondering how he could get in. Now he had a golden opportunity. 'When do you want it doing?'

'A week tomorrow.'

'The bank holiday weekend? What about a diversion?'

'Already arranged.'

'How much does Alistair know?'

An odd question. 'Just that I needed someone with your skills, why?'

'I said I'd never do another job. One of these days I'll run out of luck. I want out. But who says No to Alistair'?

This was dangerous. 'You're asking me to double-cross Alistair?'

'Consider what might happen if there was, how can I put it, a break in the chain. What would it be worth? You've done all the work and Alistair takes a chunk just because … One good payday. I can disappear for good.'

'You serious?'

'You bet your sweet life.'

Alistair McGreevy was a man you did not cross. Getting it wrong did not bear thinking about. 'There's just the two of us. What did you have in mind?'

'I'm not greedy. Twenty percent?'

'If you're not being straight.' The threat implicit.

'No Vince, I am. I know I'll have to wait a few weeks but, I am serious. I want out.'

'All right. What do you need locally?'

'A power supply.'

DI Trevithick winced. Facial identification was impossible. The body, identified as Patrick Kemp by his clothing – in particular the bull's head belt buckle – hadn't improved overnight.

'Anything sensible from Cabot or his family?'

'Nothing sir. They had either learnt their lesson well or, they're telling the truth.'

'Oh well. Keep them in mind. Maybe Doctor Gledhill will provide something useful.'

Pathologist Marcus Gledhill smiled at the two police officers: Detective Constable Douglas Blake and uniformed officer Graeme Valentine, both witnessing their first post mortem examination.

'What you're saying doctor,' said DC Blake, 'Kemp died when he hit the rocks and that the evidence suggests he was dropped over the edge of the quarry landing on his front. There's no evidence that the impact was to his lower legs? Furthermore, there is no evidence that he was tied up in any way?'

'That is correct. I have taking scrapings from beneath his finger nails. There appears to be some fibrous material there. Also swabs from his mouth, nose and trachea. I will let you know the results as soon as possible.'

Superintendent Bulstrode sat back in his chair. 'He was alive at the top of the quarry. Died when he hit the rocks. No evidence of being tied up and was only a matter of a few feet from the quarry face.'

'Yes sir.'

'Wait until forensic tell us what, if anything, the material taken by Dr Gledhill is.'

It took two full days to crate all the goods removed from the cellar and a further day to have them transported to Liverpool for shipment.

Later that evening Vince Cabot collected his cellar key and copy from locksmith Gregory Jones.

Wednesday, Bill Nolan helped Vince and David to start the transfer of articles from the barn to the shop.

Thursday 11.00am. Vince Cabot looked at the man standing in the entrance to his barn: Fortyish. Six feet two. Lean. Muscular. Thinning blond hair. Old razor scar from his left eye to the point of his jaw. 'We've met before,' said Vince.

'Aye,' the man replied. His smile didn't make him look any more handsome but his accent took him north of the border. 'That we have.'

He furrowed his brow studying the unwelcome face. 'Strangeways. But that must have been what? Twenty years ago.' Vince Cabot's eyes narrowed. There could be problems ahead. 'You're Ben McGreevy, Alistair's cousin.'

'Aye,' the stranger smiled again. 'Alistair said you'd as like need a hand.'

'Well, there's only Bill and me. Another pair of hands is welcome.' He stepped forwards and offered his hand. 'Have you somewhere to stay,' he said, knowing what the answer would be.

'Alistair said you'd plenty of room at the farm. Keep it cosy.'

'Not a problem. Come on we'll find you a bed.'

'And you found this by accident?' said Ben McGreevy looking at the bricks stacked in the tunnel. 'How far back are we? It seems a hell of a long way.'

'Beyond the service road. I was levelling the floor when I hit it. Mind your head. Roof's unstable, won't take much to bring the lot down. I'll show you.'

'And you reckon that's the bank?' McGreevy pointed up the stairs five minutes later.

'Yup, 283 yards down here. 300 paces in the street. Same bearing.'

'Nolan reckons he can blow it?'

'He does.'

'Where do you get the power.'

'Side tunnel back there,' he pointed over his shoulder. 'Leads to the parish church.'

'The Archdeacon? Gordon told me about him. You've got a surprise for him. If it've been up to me I've have floated him down the Clyde. Less messy.'

'Well, what I've got planned will put him inside. He'll suffer in there.'

'As you wish.'

'I do. One more point Ben. No talk at home. Vanda and the children know nothing of this. My daughter just got married and her husband is a complete innocent. He's clever and a good lad. I want them kept out of this. Is that clear?'

Vance saw the look. McGreevy didn't like being told what to do. So be it.

Bulstrode put the file on his desk, leaned back and looked at the three officers. 'So, the fibres under Kemp's nails were carpet fibres, believed red in colour. There were also similar fibres recovered from his mouth, trachea, and lungs.' He turned his attention to Douglas Blake. 'You've been to Cabot's farm?'

'Yes sir. There was no trace of any red carpet.'

'Nevertheless, pay another visit. Check it thoroughly. Make sure. Roberts, you go with him. Two pairs of eyes are better than one.'

'Before they go, sir,' said DI Trevithick. 'Blake was telling me that he saw Sandra Montgomery and Beryl Newsome, girlfriends of Baler and Smith, coming out of Galbraith's.'

Bulstrode frowned. 'I can't believe they've anything of their own that might interest Galbraith. So what?'

'I agree sir,' said Douglas Blake. 'They'd been buying. Unredeemed pledges. Montgomery had bought a gold wrist bangle and Newsome a gold necklace and crucifix. £10 each.'

Bulstrode started. 'Where in heaven's name did they get that sort of money?'

'They say from Baler and Smith, sir. I checked it with Galbraith. As usual no questions asked. But, all through the books. As to where the money came from?'

'Trevithick, get hold of these two and find out whilst Roberts and Blake check out the farm.'

Vanda Cabot was frightened. She hadn't liked this Scottish stranger at first sight.

Whilst Vince was showing him round the farm it took five seconds to find the sawn-off shotgun and cartridges at the bottom of his bag. What the Hell was Vince up to? Who was this Ben and what did he want?

'Do you want tea or something stronger, Vince?' Vanda called when she heard the door open.'

'Forget the tea, Vanda.'

'I thought you might say that. Steak for tea. Ready in Twenty minutes. Celeste and David will be here.'

'David, ya canna say that. A kirk is what you sassenachs call a church. Always has been.'

Vince slid silently into the room and into his chair. He hadn't been missed. When Vanda told him about the shotgun he was furious. With a family as volatile as the McGreevys, a loose cannon with his own artillery was not a good idea. With the whisky flowing after the meal Vince had risked paying a visit to Ben's room and spent five minutes with a rasp doctoring the twin firing pins, collecting the filings on a piece of paper and wiping the pins before replacing the gun in Ben's bag.

He sat back smiling. David was a light drinker. Although he liked a drink and was now relaxed and happy. Ben, on the other hand, drank whisky like pop. He was in a good mood.

It had been a revelation. Ben had taunted David because he studied archaeology. However, David had spent a lot of time studying the Romans in what is now Scotland, around north Glasgow and the Antonine Wall and Bar Hill Roman Fort., situated south of the River Kelvin and north of the Forth and Clyde canal; between Auchinstarry in the east and Twechar in the west. "No so bad, an Englishman that knows something about Bonnie Scotland, other than the whisky"

David held his hand up. 'No, Ben it hasn't, look.'

Vanda and Celeste stood in the doorway. 'Does he usually drink whisky?'

'No, just beer and not much at that.'

'He's going to have one hell of a head in the morning.'

David flicked through Vince's road atlas opening it at the map of Great Britain. 'Look Ben, this is Great Britain.'

'Naw, Greater Scotland,' he said with an inane grin.

'Have it your way but this is it,' he pointed to each in turn. 'Scotland, England, and Wales. First we have to go back to the Romans.'

'What's it got to do with the Romans?'

'Remember, there's a Roman fort at Bar Hill.'

'Aye. So? ...'

'... Kirkintilloch means Fort at the head of a hill. It comes from Scottish Gaelic, Caer, meaning a fort. Over time Caer became Kirk. Cinn meaning at the head of. And Tulaich meaning a hill.

Caer cinn tulaich - Kirkintilloch. It's the progressive changes in languages over time.

A loud knocking at the door ended the conversation. 'I'll get it,' said Vanda.

'Sergeant Roberts,' said Vanda. 'I don't recognise your friend.'

'DC Blake, Mrs Cabot,' he showed his warrant card. 'Could we come in? We need a word with Vince.'

'Of course,'

A *shocked* Vince Cabot looked across the kitchen table at the two officers. 'Where?'

'The quarry at Barnaby Glen,' said Blake, 'Although there wasn't much of his face left. But he had that distinctive bull's head belt buckle. His father identified that and his clothing. As you were one of the last to see him alive we'd like another look around your farm.'

'Yeah, whatever. Look, I won't pretend I'm sorry, he was a nuisance especially if you had a daughter. I'll have to see Quincy he'll be torn ... Sorry, where do you want to start?'

Vince Cabot and Ben McGreevy watched as the rear lights of the car disappeared. 'Did they find anything?'

'There was nothing to find, Ben,' he said. 'But I guarantee they'll be back. Why the hell did you tell them your name was McGarvie?'

'Pah. English police, they don't know me.'

'There's a new invention called a telephone.' He pointed at Ben's face. 'One call to Glasgow and that scar will identify you. They'll be back and with luck it'll be tomorrow. I've got to get you away, now.' He glanced over his shoulder at Vanda.

'I'll pack him some food.'

Through the fog of whisky fumes swirling inside his head Ben McGreevy was struggling to understand. 'I'm not going anywhere, Vince.'

'You bloody well are and now. I'm taking you to the shop. You'll be all right there. I've got things to sort out. Bill and me'll be there later tomorrow. Just keep your fucking head down. Get your bag.' Bloody idiot.

'There's something wrong there, Sarge. Did you see Vince Cabot's face when that other man gave the name McGarvie.'

'I did. And that tale about him travelling to the Birmingham area to find some lost relative and just stopping off at Cabot's over night? Stinks. When we get back come to my office and get the almanac. Call Glasgow. See what they have to offer.'

'Good morning DC Blake. And what can we do for you this morning.'

'I called last night but someone suggested I call back this morning.'

'Did they say why?'

'No. Just that I should call back. But seeing we're talking, does the name Ben McGarvie mean anything?'

'McGarvie? The only McGarvie that we might have been interested in died last year. Or, rather succumbed to a knife wound. Can you describe whoever it is you're interested in?'

'His main identifying feature would be an old scar, by the corner of his left eye ...'

'And runs down to the point of his jaw. Six feet two, boney, blond hair aged around forty?'

'That's him.'

'He have a bag with him?'

'Yes.'

'His name's Ben McGreevy. Carries a shotgun and will use it. His cousin, Alistair McGreevy, is doing ten in your neck of the woods for robbery with violence. He's due out in a few weeks. But if Ben is there you'd better be on the lookout.'

'Right, I'll see to that. Before I go have you any outstanding warrants?'

'Not sure. I'll call you back in about thirty minutes.'

Bulstrode sat bolt upright. 'Shotgun!'

'Yes sir,' said Blake. 'And if it's in the bag I saw it's a sawn-off.'

'Christ.' The sweat stood out on his brow. 'Trevithick, draw firearms.'

DI Trevithick addressed the six officers. Four issued with revolvers and six rounds. The two remaining had their own Lee-Enfields.

'Last night a man by the name of Benjamin 'Ben' McGreevy stayed with Vince Cabot at his farm. McGreevy reputed to be in possession of a sawn-off shotgun. The object is to secure any unlawfully held firearms and arrest McGreevy; without the need to open fire.

There are innocent people at the farm. As far as we know Mrs Vanda Cabot and her married daughter Celeste and Celeste's husband David Thomas.

Bill Chapman, the local Pc will meet us there. Any questions? No? Good.

It was teeming down. Not the day to be standing in the rain if you could avoid it.

'Everyone in position, Sergeant?'

'Yes sir.'

'What's he really like, Chapman?'

'Vince Cabot? As a youngster he was a tearaway. Did time. When he met Vanda it was like throwing a switch. Never been in trouble since and that's over the past twenty years. Don't get me wrong, sir, he can look after himself. But I've known him all his life. I can't see him getting mixed up with anyone waving a shotgun about.'

Trevithick nodded and lifted the horn to his lips. 'Mrs Cabot. Mrs Vanda Cabot, come out of the house with your hands up. Mrs Cabot.'

Five seconds later the door opened slowly and a tentative Vanda Cabot, holding an umbrella, emerged. 'If you're looking for the

Scotchman he left last night. There's just me. Celeste and David are in their cottage.'

'Where's your husband?'

'Vince dropped Ben off at the railway station, then went to see someone on business.'

'Who, Mrs Cabot?'

'I don't know. You'll have to ask him. Look, why don't you come in out of the rain.'

The cottage door opened Celeste and David clearly visible. 'Mum, what's up?'

'I don't know, love. The police seem to want to speak to Ben.'

'He was funny.'

'Because he was drunk. Look, come inside. If you want to check the farm and the cottage help yourselves. David, come in you look terrible.'

'What's the matter with him.'

David Thomas, his eyes deep in his head looked ninety. 'I don't drink whisky, DC Blake.'

'He did last night,' said Celeste putting her arm round his shoulders. The comment brought a laugh from the officers.

Three minutes later they were on their way.

'Do we know where McGreevy went, Trevithick?'

'There were no trains from Pontefract yesterday evening, sir. Enquiries from both Wakefield Westgate and Kirkgate are negative, but it was quite busy so it is possible that he did buy a ticket. We've got ongoing enquiries with the Transport Police and Birmingham City. In addition, a telex requesting obs. has been distributed to all forces in the north and midlands. Other than that ...?'

In the back room of The Barge Vince Cabot buttonholed Twine and Smithy. 'You think you're big enough to play with the grown-ups?'

'Of course we are,' said Twine. Smithy agreed.

'First things, understand this, you haven't seen me for the last week. No matter what you hear or read in the papers, forget it. All right?'

'Sure. But what?' said Smithy.

'Nothing to do with you. No matter what. No matter who asks the questions you know shit. Clear? Because if you do talk there will be repercussions. That means you get seriously hurt. Understand?'

There was a tentative agreement from both.

'You don't sound too certain. If you want to play it's time to show some balls.'

'Yeah, we're fine.'

'Just remember what I said. Hail rain or snow. Eight o'clock on the Heath. How you do it is up to you. Make it realistic and when the police arrive keep it going. All right?'

'Yeah, we can do that.'

'Good, here,' he gave them £25 each. 'Out the back door and go separate ways. Do not talk to each other. Keep your girlfriends apart, you know how they can gab. And don't splash the cash, you draw attention to yourselves. Remember eight o'clock, do not be late. Go.'

After almost twenty hours of being confined to Cabot's cellar Ben McGreevy was going stir-crazy. 'How fucking long before we begin. I've had enough of this.'

Vince Cabot checked his watch. 'Twenty minutes. Then we go.'

'Why can't we go now?'

'Ben, we're less than 100 yards from the police station. That's why. Now relax. Is all your gear ready, Bill?'

Bill Nolan wanted to get as far away from any member of the McGreevy family as he could, and as soon as possible. He nodded. 'Everything's in the tunnel, Vince.'

'Right, we go.' Vince Cabot followed by Bill Nolan and Ben McGreevy bringing up the rear set off along the tunnel. One minute later Cabot took hold of one end of the power cable heading for the cellar door of All Saints. Bill Nolan the other end heading for the staircase.

Vince had tried the new key just to make sure. After filing the edges it worked perfectly.

Voices! Who the hell was in the church at this time on a Saturday? Bloody Hell. Easter Sunday tomorrow. Christ.

Cable down he crept to the top of the stairs. There was a meeting in Desmond's office. Four perhaps five people. It didn't sound as though they were getting ready to leave.

'What are you doing back here, there's no power?'

'There's a meeting in the church office, Bill. I can't get to the socket.'

'What the fuck do we do next? I can shift them.'

'Ben, the idea is that we conclude our business without arousing suspicion. This cable is almost 400 yards and, I've got an extension. Wait here.'

The moon was full although rain was forecast and the clouds were gathering. The north wind making its presence felt.

Bulstrode was concerned. 'What's brought this on, Inspector? It's been relatively quiet for six months or more.'

'I wish I knew, sir,' said Inspector Groves. 'Baler and Smith have been reported as being friendly towards each other, which we hoped was good news. But this ... There must be almost forty. If this rain would start it might dampen their ardour for a scrap.'

'Sergeant, did you ring round?'

Sergeant Edward Perfect grimaced. He would retire in four weeks. The idea of getting involved in a mass brawl with two gangs of idiots who were winding each other up was not his idea of a quiet 2-10 shift. 'Yes, sir. Everywhere is busy but there should be at least another ten en route and Force Control have promised at least four cars. Whether they are double-manned or not they couldn't say.'

'One thing sir,' said DS Greaves. 'I can't see Baler or Smith anywhere.'

'Really?' said Bulstrode. 'I wonder ...'

Before he could continue a piece of brick could be seen arching across the sky. The scream indicating that someone had been in the way.

'Good God,' Inspector Groves flinched as a hail of missiles from both sides began.

It took fifteen minutes to reach his office and find his extension cable, plug the extension lead in and run through the trapdoor and get back without anyone from the Coach And Horses opposite seeing him through the shop window.

The cable reached. But only just.

'It's not ideal,' said Bill. 'But it'll have to do.'

In the confines of the staircase and the tunnel the noise was deafening. The cement dust blinding. No-one had thought of dust masks or goggles. Nevertheless, with the hammer drill progress was good.

'That should do,' Bill Nolan stepped back and put the drill down. 'How late are we?'

'Twenty five minutes. I'll just check the church again. You get set up.'

The church was in darkness. Nevertheless he locked the door on the way back.

'It's clear. Have you done enough?'

'Blow it now,' demanded McGreevy. 'We've waited long enough.'

'We should be ok, Vince. It just depends how much reinforcing there is.'

'Patience, Ben. Rushing will only get us nicked. Ok Bill blow it. We've got bolt croppers just in case.'

The blast brought the tunnel down.

It took a while but eventually there were eighteen police officers. There had been a few rioters that broke away when the police cars arrived but most persevered.

Superintendent Bulstrode placed his prisoner in the van. 'You look as though you've enjoyed yourself, sir,' said Douglas Blake.

'Indeed I have, Blake,' he said wiping the blood from his nose. 'How many in total?'

'Twenty two, sir. We know who most of the others are but no sign of Twine or Smithy. The magistrates will be busy on Tuesday.'

Superintendent Bulstrode stopped dead in his tracks. 'Explosion?'

'Yes sir. Mind you he was a bit worse for wear. Said he felt a vibration in the pavement when he was passing the bank and heard what he described as a muffled explosion.

The building is secure. The keyholder hasn't arrived yet. Although he poo-pooed the idea.'

'Very well, Sergeant. Keep me informed.'

Dust and debris was everywhere. 'What the fuck happened, Bill, are you ok?'

'Yeah,' croaked Bill. 'Keep your cap on and your mouth and eyes closed until the dust settles.'

'Ben. Where's Ben?'

'Don't know. He left the side tunnel.'

It took five minutes before the dust settled. 'By, don't you look a bonny bugger, Vince?' laughed Bill.

'You could be mistaken for the abominable snowman. What happened?'

'I thought the drilling was going well. Too well. Look at this,' he bent down and picked up a lump of what looked like concrete. 'Watch.' Bill Nolan used his thumb and the object collapsed into powder. 'This is not concrete. No hard core. It's just mortar. And a weak mix at that.'

'Let's see what the damage is. And where's Ben?'

They found him ten yards away. 'That doesn't look good.' Ben McGreevy was lying on his back. He had caught a brick full in the face. 'He can't help anymore.'

'What do we do with him?'

'Put him down the corridor next to the door until we're ready to go. Grab his legs.'

Ben McGreevy was safely out of the way. 'Right let's see what we have.'

The steps were clear and access to the vault now simple. There was as much damage above ground as below.

'Where do we start?'

'I'll start this side, Bill. You take the other. Cash, bullion, jewels, documents and small objects. If you find any decent looking jewellery let me see. I have to leave a present for the archdeacon.'

'Why him?'

'Because he owes Gus Roberts a small fortune. And he interferes with kids. When the police find it in his safe ...'

'Gotcha.'

It was slow but satisfying. One-by-one the coal sacks were filled and taken to the tunnel.

Geoffrey Wideman, the manager of the Northern General Bank unlocked the door and stepped back to allow DS Roberts access to the vault anteroom. Wideman followed. 'I told you Sergeant,' he said examining the door of the vault. 'Not a scratch. There's nobody been in this room since 2.30pm on Thursday and there will be nobody in here until Tuesday next at 9.30am. This is as safe as the Bank of England. Unless,' he chuckled, 'you are suggesting that a team of coalminers burrowed their way through the foundations.'

Every box ransacked. Bill's drill and Ben's bag complete with shotgun in the tunnel waiting for Sunday night.

'I'm knackered, Vince. How much longer?'

'Not long, Bill. We need to get the cable out from under this rubble. That goes into the church with everything else. And I put this beauty into the safe,' he pulled the emerald necklace from his pocket.

'That's beautiful. Pity we have to give it away.'

'There's plenty more Bill. Don't worry. Small sacrifice. Keep everything together. Don't want the police looking for missing essentials.'

Twenty four hours later. The loot sorted into biscuit boxes and buried inside of the step, surrounded by several layers of brick. Ben McGreevy's body laid in the cellar along with the cable, drill and bolt cutters. The original cellar key and the emerald necklace secreted at the back of the archdeacon's safe. Vince and Bill exited the cellar locking the door. Washed in the toilet sink. Working clothes in a sack. They dressed.

'My job is to tell Gordon about Ben. That I don't look forward to.'

'I don't envy you that.'

'Can't leave it until it breaks he'll draw the right conclusion. And you're ok for Gordon's welcome home present?'

'You can count on me, Vince. Fear not.'

'You got enough money to tide you over?'

'Yes, I'll keep my head down. Don't worry.'

'I've got your address and you know where I live. Be careful and we all win.'

Bill Nolan out of the way Vince Cabot returned to the tunnel. It took an hour before he removed the last of the boxes and replaced the bricks. The journey to his farm north of Grassington took two hours. He arrived as Gustav was about to begin milking. 'You need help with that chest, Vince?'

'Please,' he said. 'Easier with two.'

Chest secreted he handed Gustav ten £1 notes and tapped him on his shoulder.

'How long you stay for?'

'Two days. Now I'd like to get some sleep.'

'Good. Katharine she is cooking breakfast. Good to eat. Sleep better.'

'Get that phone, Blake. Then it's time for court.'

He grinned. 'Yes, Sarge,' he picked the phone up. 'Sergeant's office, DC Blake.'

'The bank's been robbed. Everything's gone.'

He lifted his hand and snapped his fingers. 'Whoa. Steady. Who are you please and which bank?'

'Mr Wideman, Manager of the Northern General. Hurry.'

They stood and stared at the destruction. The remains of the floor and the forced security boxes. No trace of any contents.

'Good God.'

'Saturday evening Sarge. Report of that explosion. At least we did check out the report. Look in the corner.'

The hole beckoned like a crooked finger.

'Are you OK to check it out whilst I make the call?'

'Yes, Sarge. I've got my torch.'

'Be careful.'

Blake pulled his torch from his pocket and directed the beam down the hole. 'There are steps here. What do you know about them?'

'Nothing officer. I've been here for fifteen years. I'd no idea.'

With great care Blake descended the stairs although in his considered opinion there was no chance of anyone remaining in the area. A tunnel? Four feet wide and high enough to stand straight. Blocked to the right. Debris to the right and downhill. It looked as though the roof had collapsed. Due to age or the explosion? Total blockage ahead and a side tunnel which led to a door beyond which were raised voices.

'Archdeacon Tempest, what do you mean you have sold the redundant furniture? And kindly explain why there is a dead body behind you.'

Blake thumped on the door twice with a side of his fist. 'I'm Detective Constable Blake. Open this door please.'

'Archdeacon, the key?'

'We don't have a key. It's only recently I came down here.'

'Who are you?'

Suffragan Bishop Bertram Westinghouse and Archdeacon Desmond Tempest.'

'And there is a body there?'

'There is. A very dead body with massive head injuries.'

'Which church are you in?'

'All Souls.'

'Stay exactly where you are. I'm coming round.'

DS Greaves stepped off the bottom step as Blake arrived. 'Where are you going to in such an all-fired hurry?'

'The main tunnel is blocked but there's a side tunnel that leads to All Souls where they have a corpse with massive head injuries. And there was a row ongoing between an archdeacon and suffragan bishop.'

'Isn't there a door?'

'Yes, but it's locked and they claim there isn't a key.'

DS Greaves chuckled. 'Magic. The Lord moves in mysterious ways.'

DI Trevithick looked down at Ben McGreevy. 'Is he the one, Blake?'

'Yes sir. That scar is unmistakable. Ben McGreevy, although he gave me the name McGarvie. Now we know why'

'Have you checked his bag?'

'Not as yet, sir.'

The detective inspector motioned with his head.

Bishop Westinghouse was worried. 'There is something we ought to know?' he said as Blake bent to unzip the holdall.

'Yes, Your Grace. This man is a violent criminal from Glasgow who was seen in the area last week. We were given to understand that he was leaving to travel to Birmingham. However it seems his plans changed and he is now here, in your church. The safety deposit vault in the bank at the end of the tunnel through that door was ransacked over the weekend. There are some serious questions to be asked.'

'Surely, you do not suspect involvement by members of this congregation?'

'It's here sir,' said Blake holding the sawn-off shotgun by the end of the barrel to the shock of the two clergymen.

'We follow the evidence Your Grace. And, at the moment it led us here.'

There was a soft click. 'Use your handkerchief, Blake, put the cartridges in here,' DS Greaves passed him an evidence bag. 'Whilst we await the photographer shall we repair to your office?'

'How many keys to your safe, Archdeacon?'

'But surely ..'

'Archdeacon, the detective inspector will want to eliminate the church from their enquiries, please hand them your key. There is only one key here Detective Inspector. There is a spare in Diocesan Office.'

'Blake.'

'What should there be in the safe, Your Grace?'

'Papers relating to All Souls. Monies. Just the usual things you might expect, officer.'

One article at a time Blake emptied the safe. 'Sir,' he past the DI the key.'

'I've never seen that before,' protested the archdeacon.'

'Sergeant,' he passed the key to DS Greaves. 'This looks old enough to fit the door in the cellar.'

The DS disappeared down the cellar steps as DC Blake looked up at the archdeacon. 'Do you keep any jewellery in your safe?'

The archdeacon froze.

'Archdeacon?' queried the Bishop. 'Answer the officer.'

'No. Jewellery? Why would I?'

'You stated that you had the only key,' said Blake.

'Yes, but why are you asking?'

'Sir.' Blake stood and handed Vince Cabot's present to DI Trevithick.

DS Greave re-appeared. 'It's a perfect fit, sir. The door is open.'

'I don't understand.'

'It's quite simple, Archdeacon. At some time between last Friday and now. Using the tunnel you can access via your cellar. We believe Saturday evening. Persons as yet unknown gained access to the security vault of the Northern General Bank. They ransacked the private security boxes then made good their escape. It is probable that the man in your cellar was involved. If you cannot provide an explanation as to your possession of that key and where this, what appears to be an emerald necklace, came from then I must draw the obvious conclusion. Blake.'

'Sir.' Blake faced the archdeacon. 'Desmond Tempest you are not obliged to say anything unless you wish to do so but anything you say may be used in evidence.' Blake put his hand on the archdeacon's shoulder. 'I am arresting you on suspicion of the burglary of the Northern General Bank.'

The archdeacon looked sick. 'I, I don't understand.'

'Detective Inspector, before you remove the archdeacon would it be possible to see this tunnel to which you refer?'

After a four hour sleep Vince Cabot woke. Washed and went to the hay loft. Behind the bales he unlocked his chest settling back to check the documents removed from the vault. Cash and jewellery were one thing. Paper could be far better. He wasn't disappointed. Much of it was not his speciality, but there were those who would pay for what he could not use. However, bearer bonds were a different kettle of fish. Whoever possessed them owned them. These were particularly interesting, less than five months to redemption. These he would keep. There would be more than enough to split with Bill, providing the second stage of his plan went smoothly.

Everything secured it was time to catch up with Gustav and Katherine, now only two months before her big day.

The atmosphere in prison was never good, unless you were leaving.

'Vince? I never expected to see you so soon. Problem?'

He was volatile at the best of times how he would react to the death of his cousin was anybody's guess. 'Yes. Your cousin paid us a surprise visit. Brought his favourite toy with him.'

'What?'

'He said you'd told him I'd need a hand.'

'What the fuck does he think he's playing at. Wait 'til I get out.'

'Now, that is a problem. You know how impetuous he could be. He liked to play with fire.'

'Burned?'

'Permanently.'

Alistair McGreevy threw his head back and laughed. 'Serve the silly bastard right. And?'

'The archdeacon will look after him.'

'Brilliant.'

'I'll fill you in fully in a few weeks. I haven't had time to have a proper look. Have to wait until the weather is cooler. News hasn't got out yet. So...'

'Once he's identified I'm sure to get a visit. And they'll see your name on the register.'

'If I'd used it they might. But they'll still be here within the next few days.'

'And Bill. Is he ok? I heard a whisper that he was planning to move house.'

'I've not heard anything and he hasn't said anything. But he's quite happy with what I gave him.'

McGreevy grinned across the table. 'Good. Always happy when your team play ball. You still take holidays in the farm above Kettlewell?'

Vince Cabot frowned. It didn't matter how he knew about Kettlewell, he did. Thanks for the warning. He didn't know about the others. 'From time-to-time I do. Nice place.'

Yes, you bastard, thought McGreevy, I know you of old. 'I've told you Vince. I know everything. Well if there's nothing else, Vince. I'll see you in a few weeks. Get the champagne on ice.'

'Alistair, you can count on it.'

'Before we go into the tunnel, sir. When I first came to the door I overheard a vigorous discussion between the Bishop and the Archdeacon regarding some missing furniture.'

'That can wait, Blake.'

'Detective Inspector,' said the Bishop. 'It might be relevant to the archdeacon's misdeeds. He was very short on details when the matter first arose. Some of the furniture here was very old and may be valuable.'

DI Trevithick turned the Archdeacon. 'Care to enlighten us?'

'I had a visit from a local antique dealer, Vince Cabot ...'

'Cabot, you know Vince Cabot?'

'Yes, he knew more than I did about the furniture in here. He told me he had helped Father Casey at English Martyrs and Reverend Wilkins at St. Catherine's. I checked and they were delighted with the results.'

'And he bought it?'

'No, Your Grace. It's gone to New York to be auctioned.'

'What?' was the astounded response. 'And you authorised this?'

'Well, yes. He said he couldn't do it without a signature or people might think he had stolen it.'

'And you have a copy of this agreement?'

'Of course, it's in the safe.'

'I will deal with this later. You have no authority to dispose of anything belonging to the church. Your financial remit concerns only day-to-day finance. And what does this Cabot gain from this transaction?'

'20% of the hammer price and he pays all the expenses including shipping.'

If looks could have killed. 'Very well. Thank you Inspector.' The archdeacon was very concerned. Was Vince Cabot involved? But how? And how in the name of God could he get out of this mire? As for Gus Roberts. He didn't want to think about him at all. But couldn't get the face out of his mind.

'Blake, have you got your torch?'

'Yes, Sarge? Mind your feet gentlemen there's a lot of rubble about.'

It had taken Vince Cabot and Bill Nolan over thirty minutes to block the tunnel. It wouldn't stop the police from moving the rubble but it would slow them down.

'And this tunnel leads directly to the bank vault, which was secure.'

'Correct, Your Grace.'

The archdeacon transported to the police station and booked in. The church office and cellar now out of bounds. Suffragan Bishop Westinghouse made his way to the archdeacon's home to use the telephone.

'Find Cabot and bring him in.'

Forensic scientists, pathologist, photograph and fingerprint officers in attendance. A sample from a small pool of blood found where Ben McGreevy had been standing when struck by the brick that killed him was taken for comparison.

Vince Cabot was leaving the shop. 'Vince Cabot?'

He turned and smiled which was not reciprocated. 'I am, what can I do for you officers.'

'We're taking you in for questioning re the bank robbery.'

'I've just had a call from the Northern General to say that my safety deposit box has been screwed. I'm on my way there now.'

'No, you're coming with us.'

'If you say so.'

'We do.'

Inside DI Trevithick was fuming.

'And there's nothing?'

'Not a thing, sir,' said DS Roberts. 'It sounds fishy but Cabot recently began to rent a safety deposit box and the bank had telephoned him as he said. Apparently he had £100 stashed away. The archdeacon had signed an authority for Cabot to ship the furniture to New York. There's no record at the prison that he ever visited Alistair McGreevy who had been made aware that his cousin Ben was dead and the circumstances.'

'How did he find that out? It hasn't been released.'

'He won't say. Cabot insists that he dropped Ben McGreevy off at Wakefield Westgate. Then spent a couple of days with a former German POW called Gustav Maier, at a small farm near Grassington. The locals have spoken to Maier and confirmed the story.'

'How did that happen, him meeting this Maier character?'

'Maier had been one of the first German's to be released. He'd had some kind of admin job before the war and wasn't deemed to be a risk. Had already been working as a farm labourer in that area during the war. One day he helped Cabot out when he was involved in a road accident and they became friends. Maier's never been in trouble and he married a local girl ... There's nothing in Cabot's tone or his story that doesn't tally.'

'Cabot's farm?'

'Searched again, sir. Vanda Cabot was only too willing to let us search without a warrant. That tells its own story.'

'Blake, what about Baler and Smith?'

'They've kissed and made up, sir, or so they claim. Their sheep wanted a swan song. Last Saturday was it. As far as they are concerned they're saying nothing. There was that report from those two drunks of an explosion as they walked passed the bank. That was checked out. I don't believe for one second that the scrap on the heath wasn't staged to coincide with the raid on the bank and keep us tied up.'

'Right, what have we missed?'

'Cabot, sir,' said Blake. His fingers are everywhere in this. He knows the archdeacon and he's been in the cellar. He knows the door exists. Within the last month he rented a box from the bank. McGreevy was at his house two days prior to the raid. And, don't you think the evidence is a bit too obvious – the key and the necklace being in the safe? McGreevy's body in the cellar? Nobody is that stupid.'

'Could be just plain hubris, Blake. I'm a man of the cloth who would suspect me.'

'True, sir. And the key. Is there another one? If not they would have to have made good their escape via the front or side doors and carry their loot away with the risk of being spotted.'

'You're suggesting that they used the tunnel to escape?'

'It's a possibility, sarge. But which way?'

'Fair point.'

'But if it was Cabot, why would he frame the archdeacon? They appear to get on well.'

'There you have me, sir. It was just a thought.'

DI Trevithick collected his thoughts out of the window. 'Blake, here,' he handed him the cellar key. 'Take this and physically check every locksmith within a ten mile radius. See what you can find.

'Sergeant, contact the Mines Rescue and ask someone to come and have a shufty at this brickwork. If it's all right, get some overalls and organise a team to begin clearing the tunnels. Start on the top side see where it leads. If that draws a blank, downhill.'

Once again free, Vince Cabot set about levelling the shop's cellar floor. The last load of concrete had been poured. All he had to do was to finish off then leave it. Strong enough to walk on in a week but it would take a month to fully cure.

'Hello,' DC Blake's voice from the shop. 'Anybody there? Vince, Vince Cabot?'

The thought what does he want now? Ran through his brain. Without thinking he shouted, 'I'm in the cellar. Don't come down unless you want concrete over your shoes. Nip upstairs and put the kettle on I'll be with you in two minutes.' The thunderbolt hit. 'Christ. The carpet.'

Changing his shoes he crept up the stairs. If the gas-ring had been lit it would have been roaring. Silence.

Blake was on his knees putting something in an envelope which promptly disappeared into his pocket.

'Nice carpet,' said Cabot. 'Bought it in an auction some time ago.'

Blake struggled to his feet, turned and smiled. 'I was just thinking it would look nice in our living room. I shall have to keep my eyes open.'

He saw the look on Blake's face. Does he know?. 'Is there something I can help you with that you couldn't ask whilst I was in custody?'

Blake smiled. 'Touché. Yes, there is. You, according to Archdeacon Tempest, had known him for quite a long time and were on good terms. Is there anything you can think of why he would be short of money? Something that might tempt him to get involved in a venture like the raid on the bank?'

Cabot feigned disbelief. 'He was involved in that? The bastard's got my money? Good God, I wouldn't have believed it. But to answer your question. He liked the gee-gees. There were rumours floating round that he was in hock to Gus Roberts who as beginning to fret.'

'Do you know how much?'

'It was rumoured to be a lot, but you'll have to ask Gus.'

'I will. That was what I wanted to ask. So I'll decline your offer of tea and be on my way.'

You stupid bastard, Vince said to himself. *Their scientists must have found carpet fibres on Kemp's body. The only reason he would want some would be for comparison. You stupid bastard.*

Vince Cabot sat heavily in the chair facing his solicitor, George Rutherford.

'Not like you to look worried, Vince. Tell me everything?'

... A wide-eyed George Rutherford leaned back in his chair, exhaled and picked up the phone. 'Coffee for two please, Cath. Vanda and the children all right?' he said as he put the phone down.

'They're fine. Celeste is beginning to show. I think she and David will make a good couple.'

'Good.' The door opened. 'On my desk please.'

'Right,' he said as the door closed behind his receptionist. 'How do you feel about prison?'

'Not enamoured. But better than being hanged.'

Rutherford smiled. 'It would never have come to that. But I think your memory is failing you, Vince.'

'How so?'

'In spite of his unwanted advances to your daughter you had no intention of killing Kemp, had you? The answer is, No.'

'No.'

'Good. Neither had you any intention of causing grievous bodily harm.'

'I did not.'

'Excellent. What you intended to do when you tied him up, and that is kidnapping by the way, was to frighten him into understanding that his continued approaches towards your daughter would no longer be tolerated.'

'Yes, I see what you mean. That's exactly what I hoped for.'

'And, you also intended to roll him over the cliff at the other side of the quarry, where the drop is much less. He would have fallen into several feet of water and would have been able to scramble out. When you realised your mistake you panicked and why you lied to the police.'

'True.'

'You have details of the girls Kemp defiled?'

'I have.'

'Excellent.' Rutherford removed several sheets of blank cream wove and a sheet of carbon paper from his desk drawer, interleaved them and pushed them across the desk along with a ballpoint pen. 'You are going to write your statement which I will dictate.'

'Read it through and if you're happy sign it directly beneath the bottom line. Then I will witness your signature.'

'Then I have to tell Vanda and the others.'

Vanda, Celeste and David stared at him.

'Dad, what do you mean you'll be away from home for a while.'

'This is difficult. I don't want to go into details ... I was responsible for Patrick's death and I've decided to go to the police and admit what I did before they come to arrest me.'

'I don't understand.'

'Let me explain what your father told me. Even though he had expressly forbidden Patrick Kemp from approaching you, he did.'

'I know,' said Celeste. 'He wanted to marry me. Even though I was only fifteen.'

'Your father took him, or kidnapped him and took him to the quarry at Barnaby Glen and they had a row. He said he would throw Patrick in the quarry if he didn't leave you alone. Patrick refused so your father pushed him over the edge. Unfortunately where he pushed wasn't into the water as he thought. That was round the other side and he fell onto the rocks and died.'

'But doesn't that make it an accident?'

'No Celeste. It might be construed as recklessness. It could also be classed as manslaughter. That is why we have to go and tell our side of the story first.'

'Does that mean you're going to prison?'

'Yes David. Patrick Kemp had a terrible reputation in the area and Vince did what he did to protect Celeste. And, all the other underage girls in the area.'

'What are you?,' said Vanda putting her arms round his neck.

He put his arms round Vanda's waist and smiled. 'Sorry,' he said and stepped back.

'Aren't we all.'

'But what happens to the business?'

'Ah. I want you to take it over, and,' he put his hand up before David could speak. 'I heard the way you spoke with Ben last week. Your knowledge might be a bit light but with your ability you could do it. Vanda will give you all my books. My only advice is when you know the value offer them ten percent to start with and come up to twenty five percent, in easy stages if you have to. Don't be afraid to say that's all I'm prepared to offer. If they um-and-ah about our price say, Well, I could give you an additional five percent. Stick there. In my notebooks you'll find lots of examples. And in my accounts what I paid. Use that as a guide.'

'Vince, we have to go.'

'Before we go, here.' Vince handed three envelopes to Vanda, a large one for her and small one each for Celeste and David. 'And there's one for you George.'

Sergeant Paul Burrows frowned as Vince Cabot and George Rutherford entered the police station. 'Don't often see you in here, Vince,' he said.

'It's not often I need to come in, Paul.'

'What can we do for you?'

'My client, Mr Cabot and I would like to speak with Detective Inspector Trevithick.'

He had never seen Vince Cabot in the company of a brief before, never mind a slippery bastard like Rutherford. Vince was looking uncomfortable. 'Might I ask the reason?'

'We would prefer to discuss that with the detective inspector.'

DI Trevithick looked across his desk at the pair. Rutherford was well known. A good defence lawyer and for the first time since he had known him, Cabot had lost the cockiness he was noted for. 'Yes gentlemen?'

'My client, Mr Cabot, would like to accept his responsibility in the sad demise of Patrick Kemp.'

The detective inspector started. This was one for the books. 'You're admitting killing Kemp?'

'No, Detective Inspector. Perhaps you had better read this.' He removed Vince Cabot's statement from his briefcase and passed it across the desk. 'I've kept a copy.'

The DI put the statement down. A frank admission and we have nothing to gainsay. 'You're admitted tying Kemp up in your carpet until you got to the quarry. Then during an argument over his unwarranted attention to your daughter you pushed him and he fell over the edge onto the rocks. You thought that he would fall into deep water. And you did this to put the frighteners on him? You were not intending to do him any serious harm.'

'In simple terms, yes. You'll see from the statement ...'

'Yes, your daughter was one of fifteen virgins defiled by Kemp.'

'I know you have a daughter, Mr Trevithick. What would you do to protect her?'

'I understand, Mr Rutherford, but until such time as this evidence of yours is checked out, you Mr Cabot, will be staying with us on suspicion of manslaughter.'

Cabot nodded; he had expected as such. He was cautioned, searched and placed in a cell.

Blake and DS Roberts stood facing the DI. 'Blake, you saw Cabot earlier today?'

'Yes sir. At his shop which is when I spotted the carpet. I managed to obtain some fibres and sent them for forensic comparison. They will let us know tomorrow.'

Trevithick smiled. 'He came in with Rutherford and admitted tying Kemp up. Having a row over Cabot's daughter and pushing Kemp, who fell over the edge of the quarry. Get your story in first. The crafty bastard. Doesn't mean he's wrong. Still. Now, what else was it?'

'I asked Cabot if he knew the archdeacon was in debt. Apparently he gambles on the horses and is in hock to Gus Roberts.'

'That's a dangerous hobby. Any idea how much?'

'Yes sir. According to Roberts, who was being a bit coy, the archdeacon owes him over £300.'

'£300. That's a fortune.'

'Roberts thinks so and has been putting pressure on Tempest to repay. That could account for the key and the necklace. But bearing in mind the link between the archdeacon and Roberts, and, the archdeacon and the bank raid, I asked him if he was aware of a physical link between All souls and the bank. He was genuinely shocked. So were his goons, Jobson, Williams and Gregson so I obtained statements as to their whereabouts over the weekend. Just in case.'

'Excellent. And I take it there was no joy in finding anyone who would admit duplicating the key?'

'Not a dicky bird, sir. They were fascinated by the old key, but nothing further.'

DI Trevithick nodded. 'We'll give Tempest one more chance to level with us tomorrow. If he can't or won't clarify the situation to our satisfaction, charge him. Thank you Blake. Sergeant a word.'

Blake left. The DI handed Cabot's statement to DS Roberts. 'Read this and then make a start on interviewing these families. No matter how much I'd like to put Cabot behind bars for a long time I want it done properly. If he's lying about these girls I'll give him hell.

Now it made sense. How Vince came to know Arne Sigmundson she didn't know. What she did know was that Vince trusted him, to a point.

Vanda Cabot put her husband's letter on the table and transferred her attention to the Bearer Bonds. Could they really be worth a fortune?

It wasn't a love letter. Vince, as usual, had been incisive:

- Write to Arne Sigmundson, *par avion,* in New York two weeks prior to the redemption date. He will meet you at the airport.
- Two days before travel <u>first class</u> by BOAC.
- Do not let these Bonds out of your sight.
- Arne will tell you where the bank is.
- Whoever possesses these Bonds owns them so, do NOT tell <u>anyone</u> even Arne.
- Get some good clothes and luggage!!
- In New York stay at the Rooseveldt. Write to them. 45 East 45th Street New York. Book for three nights.
- It the US they're big on tipping. Leave a $1 on the pillow every day and generally 10%. Look after the taxi drivers.
- Don't forget to come home!

Phew! Ok.

Next was the large cash box. She knew of it but Vince kept

his business correspondence inside and she took no active part in the business.

Apart from the £1000 in £5 notes, there were his bank books. Vince was a good provider. There was over £7000 in his saving account. Also he had an account with First Harbour Savings and Loan bank, New York. What that contained she didn't know. What she did have were details of his bank account including the access details.

Now she needed a passport. According to Ken in the post office, the fastest way was to go to the passport office in Liverpool.

Alistair McGreevy spat on the floor as the wicket gate closed behind him.

The Humber Hawk glided to a halt. 'Good,' he said to himself. 'Somebody treating me with respect.' The driver jumped out and hurried towards him.

'Alistair, great to see you,' he held his hand out.

'Never mind that,' he brushed the hand away. 'Have you got him?'

The driver frowned and backed off. 'He's in the back.'

'Now then, Bill,' McGreevy said when the door closed. 'I know where Cabot is. Where I can keep an eye on him. Where's my money?'

'I don't know Alistair, honest.'

'Dinna lie to me you miserable little rat. Or, you'll be sorry.'

'I'm not. I know where we put it. Buried it at the back of his shop in his cellar. Your Ben knew where. But the police dug the cellar up. There was nothing there. Where he moved it to I have no idea. He paid me for what I did. It's no concern of mine.'

'It bloody well is.'

'Well, I don't know. And there's nothing that you can do to me to make me tell you. I don't know.'

'I'll enjoy finding out if you're lying.'

'You'd better hurry up then. I've got less than three months to live. Cancer. They've told me they can help with the pain but it's not going to be nice. There are ways to avoid the pain and you know I'm good at that.'

McGreevy froze. 'What do you mean?'

Bill Nolan smiled at him. 'You shouldn't have threatened to kill Mary. Won't be long now.'

'You bastard.' McGreevy screamed at the driver. 'Stop the fucking car. It's going to explode.'

The blast ripped the car apart. In seconds it was an inferno.

Mary Nolan found two envelopes. One addressed to her: *Sorry Mary, I didn't want to endure the pain. We've a bit put by and when Vince Cabot gets out he'll see you right.*

Take care of yourself.

Love Bill.

The second addressed to DI Trevithick.

Inspector,

I got a message from Alistair McGreevy. He wanted me to pull a job. Blow the security vault of the Northern General Bank. I wanted out but nobody says no to McGreevy. If I refused he threatened to have Mary killed. I had no option.

There's a tunnel leads from All Souls church in the town centre under the bank vault. The archdeacon is in deep trouble with a local bookie and he had the key to the tunnel. There was Ben McGreevy and me and a couple of lads I've never seen before. You know the outcome. There were about a dozen sacks of loot which I never saw again. Ben McGreevy caught a brick in the face so we left him for the archdeacon. He deserves all he gets. He's a reputation for molesting young boys.

When you read this you'll know what I've done. He shouldn't have threatened to kill Mary.

Bill Nolan

'That lets Cabot off the hook, sir.'

Bulstrode put the letter down. 'Looks like you're right., Trevithick.'

'I'll show it to Tempest see what sort of response it draws, especially about this allegation of interfering with boys. I'll find out from the diocese where he was before All Souls. See where it leads.'

Opulent wasn't a word that sprung readily to Vanda's lips, but this office was. William Montgomery Hennessy III, 45 year old great grandson of the founder, now Senior Vice President of the First Harbour Savings and Loan Bank of New York beamed.

She was what? Mid to late thirties. A complexion that only someone brought up in the English countryside would have. Dressed to the nines, but her hands told a different story. They reminded him of his grandmother when she worked on the family farm. The UK had survived the war but could it survive the peace? This lady would.

'Mrs Cabot, the value of those bearer bonds is very good. In fact you and your husband are now multi-millionaires,'

Vanda started. 'I'm sorry but I thought you said multi.'

The warm smile transformed into a broad grin. 'I did, Mrs Cabot. Only in dollar terms and not British pounds. Still $7,000,000 is a huge amount of money. Or, to be precise $7,383,784. In total you now have $7,583,784 on deposit. Now, we here at First Harbour Savings and Loan Bank of New York like to look after our clientele. Would you be agreeable to us offering you some advice on investments. You could be earning 4% or more.'

This was unbelievable. 'I have to fly back to England tomorrow Mr Hennessy. My daughter is expecting our first grandchild. Her husband, David, is managing my husband's business whilst he is indisposed.'

'Please, Mrs Cabot, call me William. I understand. One moment please.' He picked the phone up. 'Marcy, send Michael in please.'

Vanda yawned as the BOAC flight to London lifted off the runway. This was ridiculous. $200,000 was a fortune, but this? Lunch with Vice President and his father, President of the Company. Leaving the Bank later that afternoon with the confirmatory paperwork. She longed to see Vince's expression when she told him. At least now he was on remand she had visiting rights.

Celeste was blooming. The baby was alive and kicking. David doing well at the shop.

Dressed in her normal clothes she sat opposite Vince and put her hand on his.

The nearby prison officer snapped. 'No touching. Keep your hands back.'

Vanda blanched as she looked up. 'Sorry.'

They made eye contact and smiled. 'Well?'

'Seven,' she said.

Vince looked puzzled. He mouthed. 'Thousands?'

'Add three noughts.'

The puzzled look swiftly replaced by smiles. 'What!?'

Vanda nodded.

'Right, I want you to see Frank Nevison at The Barge, find out where Bill Nolan's widow lives. I've got his address at home but I don't know where I put it. Without him what we have wouldn't have been possible. I promised him twenty percent. She's entitled to it.'

'I'll do that. Now, how are you?'

'Bearing up. Trial date's set for six months.'

'Six months? Why so long?'

'All they'll tell me is, it's because. Can't do anything. George Rutherford's got me a KC. He reckons he's good and with those letters from the other families it won't be a heavy sentence. Just got to wait.'

'King's Counsel?'

He nodded. 'I know this is not a nice place but I'd like to see Celeste and David. In your last letter you said he was doing ok. He's a bright lad and got what it takes. And now?'

All too soon she had to leave. One last touch of hands and she was gone.

He watched as she left, turning and waving as she did so. It was meeting her almost twenty years ago that turned his life round, at least as far as violence was concerned. She never asked what he had done. He made sure that information stayed a long way from the door until the arrival of Ben McGreevy. Now the letter from Bill Nolan to the police. It was just Patrick Kemp and a charge of manslaughter.

DC Blake and DS Roberts sat opposite Archdeacon Tempest who looked worried. 'I've been charged what more do you want?'

'Desmond Tempest,' began Blake. 'You are not obliged to say anything but anything you say will be taken down in writing and may be used in evidence. This is nothing to do with the matter with which you have been charged. I understand that before you came here you was at St Xavier's in Glasgow. It was, by all accounts, a sudden move. Why?'

'Personal reasons.'

Blake nodded. 'Do you, as a minister of religion, believe that a man who knew he was going to die in the very near future would tell a lie?'

'I sincerely hope not, why?'

'Two reasons, Archdeacon, we have a document from a man now deceased, tantamount to a dying declaration, that you had been molesting boys at All Souls.'

'That's ridiculous. I admit that I gave a boy a clout for mocking me, but molestation? Certainly not.'

'Now, because of your links with St Xavier's I made enquiries with the police in Glasgow. They informed me that you moved south of the border forty eight hours after receiving a visit from one Benjamin McGreevy, the same man whose body was in the cellar at All Souls, yet you denied ever having seen the man before.'

The archdeacon felt sick. He knew what they were going to say. McGreevy had sworn the truth would be buried providing he left.

'Archdeacon, you do not look well,' said Blake. 'Perhaps you know what I am about to say?'

He shook his head. 'No, how could I?'

Blake smiled. 'The information is that the father of one of the choirboys found you in the sacristy having sexual intercourse per anum with his eleven year old son ... You don't look well. Have you any explanation?'

The archdeacon shook his head refusing to answer.

Douglas Blake was fighting to control his emotions. His son Brian was six years old. The thought that in five short years it might have been him being subjected to this. 'You don't understand?' said Blake his voice rising. 'Let me put it in the vernacular. 'You had your prick stuck up the arse of an eleven year old choirboy. In law, a child of tender years. You were fucking him. A single offence of buggery caries a fourteen year prison sentence. This was a male child you were raping. Unnatural sex. And if his father hadn't interrupted, you had sworn the child to silence on threat of hellfire and damnation if he talked. But the father went to Benjamin McGreevy, didn't he? And he paid you a visit. What have you to say?'

'It wasn't my fault.'

This was stretching credulity to breaking point. 'Are you claiming it was an accident? It was unintentional?'

'No, he was a tempter.'

Blake and Roberts looked at each other in disbelief. 'It was the boy's fault?'

'He was possessed by a demon. It was the demon that tempted me through the boy. It wasn't my fault.'

'So Archdeacon, you were tempted and failed. What did Jesus say? It would be better for a millstone to be hanged about his neck and be cast into the sea than offend one of these little ones?

'After defiling this child do you think God will welcome you when the time comes?'

There was no reply.

This conversation was bizarre. 'How often did this temptation happen ...'

Trevithick, Roberts and Blake watched whilst Bulstrode read the statements again. 'You didn't apply undue pressure, Blake?'

'No sir. I never laid a finger on him. Once we got him talking he didn't stop. Glad to get it off his chest.'

'You've got copies of the statements?'

'Yes sir,' They both replied.

'It was good work, both of you. I won't pretend I like it. I attend All Souls; it's disgusting. ... Very well. This is a Scottish offence. Get your statements typed and prepare a prosecutions file, I will have our legal department forward it to the Lord Advocate's office in Glasgow. We'll see what they can make of it. My guess is they won't find any complainants. It will disappear under the carpet. We've done what we can, well done..'

'Oh. Before you go, Sergeant, what is the present position with the bank contacting those who rented security boxes?'

'Mixed, sir. About fifty percent have been contacted and details obtained. The remainder? Some are dead; up to 20 years earlier. Their surviving relatives had no knowledge of a security box and are now scratching round for a key. Some have moved addresses and failed to notify the bank. Others for some reason claimed that the box was never used but have been paying the annual fees. Some for a long time. To be frank that beggars belief. Smells of something unhealthy. Once I have details I will instigate checks at Wakefield and Scotland Yard. Details of what we have will be circulated.'

It was just round the corner from the Barge.

Vanda rapped smartly on the door of number 31. Raised voices on the inside.

The door opened. The voices stopped. The lady was in her late forties, stout build, five feet four with permed hair her dress covered by an apron. 'Mrs Nolan?'

'Yes, who are you?'

'Vanda Cabot, could I have a word. But I heard voices. I can always come back.'

'No, please come in, I was hoping you'd call.'

The two young men looked at Vanda, 'This should be fun,' the taller of the two said to the other.'

'These two were just leaving,' she said indicating.

'We're going nowhere until we get what's ours.'

'I haven't a clue what you're talking about, now leave.'

'I'm Vanda Cabot,' she began.

'We know who you are, lady. Your old man's in clink there's nowt he can do. We're staying.'

Vanda's eyes narrowed. 'You're Baler and Smith aren't you. I've just left Frank Nevison. If you're not out of this house in ten seconds I'll fetch him. You know how persuasive he can be.'

With a bad grace they left. 'You 'aven't heard the last of this you old bag.'

'Mrs Nolan, if you see these two in the street of get harassed in any way, by them or their friends let Frank know. Now, you two, move.'

'Vanda, would you like a piece of cake. I baked it this morning.'

'I'd be delighted Mary, if it tastes as good as it smells.'

Vanda smiled and handed the letter back to Mary. 'So, Vince will see you right?

'Is it true?'

'I take it, Mary, that you knew nothing about Bill's line of work. The same as I do about my husband's businesses other than dealing in antiques.'

'Not really.'

'No, Mary. You knew nothing. He didn't involve you. You looked after the home and the children. He provided. You weren't involved in his business in any way and never asked. You had enough on your plate.'

'Yes, that's right.'

'Good. Do you have any children?'

'Three. Christopher was killed at el-Alamein.'

'I'm sorry, it must have been devastating.'

'It's still raw. They tell me time is a great healer. Not yet it isn't. And we had twin girls. They married twin Canadians at the end of the war and went back to Canada. We were planning to go and visit but now I can't see it happening. It's just too expensive.'

'Mary, do you have a passport?'

'No, we were going to get then next Spring. For the trip. But ...'

'Do you own this house?'

'No, and the landlord's put the rent up. Shortage of housing stock, he says.'

'What I'm going to tell you is a secret and must remain so. Do you understand?'

The Assize court was full. Mostly with relatives of the girls defiled by Kemp. But Vanda and David were present. Celeste was at home nursing Daniel.

'... My Lord, my client, Mr Cabot, was only doing what any decent father of a daughter would do to protect them from the ravages of a serial paedophile. Although he did not report the incident as soon as he might, he showed true contrition in handing himself into the police, and, making a full admission of his guilt. He did not try and hide, as many might. To give credit to the prosecution, they made full disclosure of the statements from the parents of Kemp's other victims asking for leniency for Mr Cabot.

I appreciate, as does my client, that his actions on that fateful night could be construed as extreme, but, I would ask that the court show leniency.'

After thirty seconds of silence Mr Justice Glendinning faced a standing Vince Cabot.

'Mr Cabot. I have weighed the facts of this case and the comments of counsel with great care. It is to your credit that you have shown contrition in your handing yourself in to the police and your plea of guilty. However, any case which comes before the court involving a death by unnatural causes must be treated with the utmost care. I understand, as the father of a young teenage daughter, your angst and your desire to take personal action against, as Sir Matthew put it, the ravages of a serial paedophile. But taking the law into your own hands must never be encouraged. In fact your admission that you forcibly subdued Patrick Kemp, tied him in a carpet before transporting him to the quarry at Barnaby Glen, is an admission of kidnapping. An offence, which in itself carries a sentence of many years in prison.'

Vanda noticed Vince's eyes drop and pallor spread across his face. 'Your action in the push, although not an attempt to push Kemp over the edge of the quarry, was, nevertheless, reckless in the extreme. The result being that the deceased died as he struck the rocks beneath. In this case there can be only one sentence. That is a lengthy term of imprisonment.' The were mutterings of disquiet from the public benches. Mr Justice Glendinning struck his desk three times with his gavel. 'Silence! Silence in court. If there are any more interruptions I will have the court cleared.' Vanda clasped David's hand as tight as she could. 'Vince Cabot, I sentence you to eighteen months imprisonment. Take him down.'

The clerk stood. 'All rise.'

Mr Justice Glendinning left the court as the public benches erupted in laughter and applause. Vince waved to Vanda. She replied and hugged David.

'I thought Vince was going to get five years.'

'So did I. But with the time he's spent inside already, and good behaviour, he could be out in less than six months.'

Marcy was escorting them along the corridor towards the office of the Senior Vice President, William Montgomery Hennessy III.

'Are you sure we're in the right place, Vanda, it's very swanky.'

'Trust me, Mary, it's right. Here we are.'

Marcy knocked and opened the door. 'Mr Hennessy. Mrs Cabot and Mrs Nolan.'

William Hennessy looked up from his desk and beamed. Stood and walked towards them.

'Vanda, how lovely to see you again.' He shook hands and turned to his left. 'And you must be Mrs Nolan,' he said, shaking hands.

'Mary, please.'

'Mary it is. Call me William. Any friend of Vanda's is welcome here. And, from the look on your face, Mary, you don't know.'

'No, she doesn't. Is everything?'

'It is. Marcy, coffee for three please. Oh, do you drink coffee, Mary?'

'I prefer tea but I do drink coffee.'

'I'll see to it Mr Hennessy.'

Coffee and tea served the small talk ended. 'Let me explain what this is all about,' said Vanda. 'The last business that Vince and Bill were involved in was very successful and beforehand, although there are no written records, Vince agreed the Bill would get 20% of the profits. We're honouring that bargain.'

'An Englishman's word is his bond?'

'It is, William. At least as far as we are concerned.'

'But what was it? Bill never spoke about what he did.'

'Vince was, in the main, a dealer in antiques although I knew he had other interests, but what they were I don't know. All I know is that the papers he asked me to deliver to William were worth a great deal of money. And you are entitled to 20%.'

'And worth much more now since the devaluation of the British pound.'

'Things are getting much more expensive, that's true. But how much are we talking about?'

'In dollar terms, Mary,' said William. 'With interest one million five hundred and ten thousand seven hundred and ninety dollars and, eighty cents.'

'I don't understand. What's that in English money?'

'A little under seven hundred thousand pounds.'

'But nobody has that sort of money.'

'You do, Mary,' said Vanda. 'Now you can afford to visit your daughters and your sister in Australia as often as you like. And all the time what you have left in the bank is earning money.'

'It's a pity Bill can't be with us. He would know what to do.'

'Your husband is ill, Mary?'

'No, William, he had advanced cancer of the bowel and in a lot of pain. He took his own life rather than suffer.'

'That is terrible. I am so sorry. Please accept my sincere condolences.'

'Thank you. He left me a letter saying that Vince would see us right. I don't think he dreamed of this.'

'Nobody did, Mary. Don't worry. It might seem like a dream but sleep on it.'

William Montgomery Hennessy III wasn't stupid. Bearer Bonds were untraceable and cash to those who possessed them. What Vince Cabot and Bill Nolan did appeared questionable? Still there was no record of any theft of that magnitude. What happened across the Atlantic was no concern of his. And, the ladies, especially Vanda, were beautiful and charming. The main thing was that commerce was flowing through his bank. Life was good.

A warrant had been obtained from a Judge in Chambers requiring the Northern General Bank to provide the full details of each security account holder. Blake, and new detective constable Graeme Valentine had been working in CRO - Criminal Record Office - checking those named account holders against the index.

'So many?' said DI Trevithick. 'Still, I don't think we should be too surprised. You and Valentine begin checks tomorrow morning.'

Vanda was determined not to cry.

George Rutherford placed a friendly hand on her shoulder.

'I'm sorry, Vanda, I really am. Vince was a great guy. It's unbelievable.'

'But what happened? He was due to be released tomorrow, I'd arranged everything. We were going to emigrate to the US, Now ....'

'As far as I can glean he stepped in when a couple of inmates attacked another. They took exception and he was stabbed with the sharpened handle of a toothbrush.'

'Yes, he always helped the underdog. There'll be an inquest?'

'There will. His Majesty's government is very keen to prevent prisoners being murdered in house.'

'Will you ...?'

'I will attend. And you?'

'Yes.'

'He left a few envelopes for you. Oh, and by the way you inherit all his property. But you already knew that.'

She nodded.

He rose and removed a box file from his safe. 'You can use the side-office. Take as long as you want. I'll send some tea in.'

She tipped everything onto the table. One envelope, not in Vince's writing, caught her eye.

There were two pieces of paper. The first a note. *'Thanks buddy. Cheque enclosed. Keep in touch.* The cheque to the amount of £650.00. The signature Damian Greatorix.

Vince had mentioned a Damian before. She would have to check.

Vince owned three farms in the Dales. One she knew about, that was Gustav, the former German POW and his wife Katharine. Why the other two? Were these where he disappeared to when he was away. Bits of country stuff he kept on the side, out of view? That would be interesting.

The others, with one exception, were to do with the various aspects of his business. One referred to a chest he had left in Gustav's barn and to treat with care. Treat with care was his shorthand for *this is expensive*. That would be first. There was also a key which she pocketed.

Documents and envelopes in her bag she went to talk with George.

'Did Vince mention that we were planning to emigrate?'

'Yes, he did. Will you still go ahead with it?'

Yes, I've spoken with officials over there and I can get sponsored. It shouldn't be a problem.'

'Do you have a timescale?'

'I think within six months.'

'Fine, what do you want to do about these farms and the antique business?'

'The farms? My gut reaction is go and see them and either give the tenants first refusal or just transfer them, basically gift them.'

'That's very generous. You sure?'

'Yes, quick and clean. I don't want any hassle.'

'As you wish. Keep me informed.'

'As far as the antiques are concerned, I have to discuss that with David and Celeste. See what they want, but first I have to tell them about Vince.'

It had not been easy. Her determination not to cry dissolved. Even David had tears in his eyes,

'It's not fair,' said Celeste, wiping her tears away. 'He was so proud when I showed him the photo of Daniel, but he never had the opportunity to hold him. What are we going to do now?'

'Well we're not going to sit down and mope. Your dad wouldn't have wanted us to do that. It wasn't him.' She turned to David. 'How long would it take you to complete your PhD?'

'Not sure. Four or five months maximum. It's mainly tidying everything up. I'll have to contact the university first.'

'That's all right. Could you do it whilst you're minding the shop?'

'Yes, and there's weekends and evenings as well. What did you have in mind?'

'I was speaking with William Montgomery Hennessy III about you the last time I was in New York.'

David and Celeste laughed. 'Who on earth has a name like that?' said Celeste.

'The Senior Vice President of the First Harbour Savings and Loan Bank of New York. One thing that the Americans don't have is a lot of history. Service by the American military over here during the war introduced them to our culture.'

'And there are a lot of rich Americans who are interested in European history, including furniture. You're thinking about expanding on what Vince did, possibly cutting out the auctions.'

'What do you think?'

'A PhD would add credibility?'

'It would. Well? Could you do it?'

'Not if I stand around talking.'

Walter arrived from university that afternoon.

They hadn't been close but he was his father. 'Will you still be going to the States?'

'Yes. Your grandmother hasn't long to live. You ought to visit her before it's too late.' He nodded. 'Apart from you two there will be nothing apart from memories. The good ones I can take with me and your father left us well provided for in America.'

'Good. I can transfer over there. There are plenty of opportunities. Far more than there are here.'

'You wish to give us the farm, Mrs Cabot?' said an astounded Gustav.

'You can buy it if that's what you prefer? But yes. Vince and I were planning to emigrate to the United States. Now that he's dead I don't want to stay here without him.'

'I would be foolish to say no. We don't know how to thank you. It was a terrible shock when we heard that Vince had been stabbed'

'Yes, it was ... And the look on your face is enough. My solicitor, a Mr George Rutherford, will be in touch. Would you mind showing me around.'

'How do you say. Last but not least. The hay barn.'

'Yes, we do ... It's very big,' said Vanda as she walked inside and looked around. So far Gustav had not mentioned anything about a chest.

'There is something here that belongs to Vince, or maybe to you. You have to climb ladder, and it is heavy.'

Lucky I'm wearing slacks, she thought.

'That's a nice chest, where did it come from?'

'Vince brought it a few weeks ago.'

Was he involved in that raid on the bank vault? The stupid bastard. 'It is heavy,' she said as she tried to lift it. 'Do you have the key?'

'Sorry, no. He did.'

'Well I haven't got it. I'll have to take it home and see if I can find it. Can we get it down?'

A rope over the beam, laced through the chest handles and tied. Balanced on the edge Vanda pushed the chest and Gustav let it run.

She took 50 x £1 notes and handed then to Gustav. 'If anyone comes and asks about Vince, he visited as the landlord, sometimes staying for a couple of days to help out. He did not bring or leave anything on your farm. It was there when you took occupation and I took it with me.'

'I understand.'

The other two farms were just that, no secret knocking shop and no property left by Vince. Two delighted tenant farmers shortly to become owners. Keep it simple.

Oh my God. 'He was involved,' she said under her breath. She stared at the bank notes. £5 and £10. Out of curiosity she picked a bundle from the top and flicked through them.

There was something odd. They had the same number. These belonged to a forger? 'I'm not risking my future. They're going no further.' Without checking further she set fire to them in a brazier until they were ash.

But why was the chest so heavy?

The answer? Five very heavy bars of gold bullion. Almost impossible for her to lift. No wonder. Vince had never mentioned gold and there was nothing in his diaries that might suggest who to contact.

'George, I'm not asking for you to divulge anything that might put you at risk. Who would Vince have contacted if he had any queries about gold bullion?'

'Very heavy?'

'Incredibly heavy. Five.'

He had a worried frown. 'I'm not telling you. It's too dangerous. But I have some papers for you to sign, I'll pay you a visit tomorrow. If you get any unexpected contacts let me know immediately.'

'Very interesting,' DI Trevithick put the report on the table and looked up at DC's Blake and Valentine. 'Just four of them have not reported any losses and don't have any previous.'

'That's correct, sir,' said Blake. 'According to the Met two of them have criminal intelligence notes linking them with a gang passing forged bank notes. The other two, associates of those who attempted a bullion heist in London two years ago. Nothing concrete.'

'Local?'

'Within a twenty mile radius.'

'That's good to know. Excellent. Draw firearms and take back-up just in case.'

Donald Rogerson smiled as he took the jewellers loop from his eye.

Superintendent Bulstrode sat back in his chair. DI Trevithick gave him a questioning look. DS Greaves, DS Roberts, DC Blake and Mary Nolan waiting in expectation.

'These are genuine, Detective Inspector. Worth a small fortune.' He looked at Mary Nolan. 'These are yours, Mrs Nolan?'

'No, I found them at the bottom of a packet of soap powder. Bill must have put them there. I don't want anything to do with them.'

'Well, I'm sure there will be a reward of some description. It's very honest of you. If there is nothing else, Superintendent.'

Bulstrode stood and shook hands. 'Mr Rogerson, thank you. DC Blake will see you out.'

Rogerson turned and handed his business card to Mary Nolan. 'Should these jewels find their way back to you and you not wish to keep them, please give me a call. Good day and good luck.'

Blake opened the door. Rogerson stepped through and stopped. 'Are you at liberty to tell me if those jewels came from the bank vault at Northern General?'

'We don't know. Mrs Nolan simply turned up with them. We will of course inform the bank. Until then. I'm afraid I can't say anything else.'

'I understand,' said Rogerson.

Blake frowned. 'Could you give me some idea as to their value?'

'A rough estimate would be £20,000.'

'Nice work if you can get it.'

'Indeed.'

Desmond Tempest appeared before the Leeds Magistrates charged with his part in the break-in at the bank and was remanded in custody. Nothing had been received from the Glaswegian Lord Advocate's office with regard to the allegations of sexual impropriety.

Vince Cabot was dead. Blake still believed that he was responsible for the murder of Patrick Kemp and his metaphorical fingerprints were all over the raid on the Vault, but now there was nothing to be done.

Bill Nolan had ruled out Cabot as being involved in the raid on the security vault. Why? His suicide taking out Alistair McGreevy and the unfortunate driver of the vehicle.

Benjamin McGreevy died in the blast at the Vault. And what was the link between Cabot and the McGreevys? Who was pulling whose strings? Too many unanswerable questions.

As for Archdeacon Desmond Tempest. He was still in denial and refusing to give any explanation for the emerald necklace and the key to the cellar door connecting All Souls to the tunnel.

Gus Roberts fumed. It was the last time he extended credit facilities to any man of the cloth.

Four months later a van from Thompson and Harland, Freight Forwarders, arrived at Vanda Cabot's farm and collected six trunks, including the one found in Gustave's barn for onward shipping to New York.

Desmond Tempest hanged himself in his cell after being informed that detectives from Glasgow were heading south to interview him.

Vanda, her son Walter and Mary Nolan slipped quietly out of the country courtesy of BOAC to start new lives in the United States.

In the meantime, David, who was expecting to hear about his PhD in four weeks, had ploughed his way through Vince's books. He wasn't about to criticise a man who had been in business for years. However, the recent devaluation of sterling against the US dollar had changed things. Prior to devaluation, $1000 raised in the US would convert to £250. $4 to the pound. Now, there were $2.50 per pound sterling. $1000 would now convert to £400. A 40% increase.

A bank transfer had been received from the First Harbour Savings and Loan Bank of New York. The total hammer price from the last consignment had realised, after deduction of commissions and taxes, $4,000.

Suffragan Bishop Westinghouse was delighted when David presented him with a cheque for £1,600.

£320 for what was now his account wasn't bad. It was when he saw an article in the times the following day that he formed the idea. Baxters, the auctioneers in Ashby-de-la-Zouche were advertising the sale of household effects of Bridgestone Manor, the country seat of Sir Montague Martindale, Bart.

He looked at the young man opposite. Antique dealers were by nature almost as old as the products they traded, this one was barely twenty three years of age.

He smiled. 'You're sure you're an antique dealer, Mr Thomas?'

David reciprocated. 'I have a degree in archaeology, Sir Montague. I'm just waiting to see if I have been awarded my PhD. My father-in-law was an antique dealer and I worked for him. Now he's dead he wanted me to take over the business.'

'I see. And you think that those who would buy my furniture at the auction will decide beforehand who gets what and not receive any counter bids?'

'I'm certain. They're hard-nosed businessmen.'

'The way of the world I suppose. You propose to buy everything outright or, ship the furniture to New York to be sold there and we divide the hammer price eighty twenty in my favour, after covering expenses.'

'Yes, Sir Montague. If I might ask did the auctioneer give you any hints as to what your furniture might achieve?'

'He told me, the market in this country in the aftermath of the war, is depressed. If it was a good day perhaps £2000 less commission.'

'Better to let the market decide rather than a group of self-interested businessmen. Sir Montague, doing it my way you know the family history and have the accounts to prove provenance. In the United States it is different.'

'You're a very persuasive young man. Just wait there a moment, please.' He left the room and seconds later. '394 please Angela ... Ah Baxter, Martindale, I've decided to cancel the auction ... No, I am positive. I've decided on an alternative ... No, my mind is made up. I'll bid you good day.'

Sir Montague Martindale was wearing a broad smile when he re-entered the library.

'Mr Baxter wasn't impressed?'

'He was not. I think that proves you were correct. Right young man. I haven't been to New York since 1931. This is your province. What do we do.'

Nothing further had been heard regarding the jewels.

George Rutherford had checked the price of gold. In The Times the price shown per fine ounce was £8.12.3d. A total value for the gold he had taken from Vanda - £18,996. He had pushed Damian Greatorix on the price as far as he could. He stuck at £12,000. Less his commission he sent a cheque to the amount of £10,800 to Vanda.

'Was that a smile or wind?'

Daniel kicked, the water splashing onto the floor as he burped. He gurgled and kicked again.

'That answers that.'

Celeste leaned forwards and kissed her son on the forehead. 'Who's a clever boy?' Daniel kicked again and waved his hand splashing more water.'

'That was a smile.'

There was a smart double rap at the door. 'See to that, David will you and don't let the cold in.'

David Thomas opened the door and took a step back. They had parted on bad terms although his father had been to the wedding and kept in touch. His mother was steadfast and refused to have anything to do with them. The last thing he wanted was a resurrection of hostilities. 'Mum, Dad?'

Martin Thomas looked at his wife. 'Lavinia?'

Lavinia Thomas was uncomfortable. She wasn't used to backing down but as Martin had drilled into her - David is our only child and

Daniel is our first grandchild. If you want a relationship with him you have to admit you were wrong. Celeste is doing a good job of being a wife and mother. He was awarded his PhD and doing well in business. You have to swallow your pride and hope that they accept. It's up to you.'

'Mum?'

Lavinia Thomas closed her eyes and exhaled. 'I'm sorry, David. Can we made amends, please.'

This was a first. He couldn't remember his mother ever apologising before. Perhaps leopards ... 'Yes, Mum,' he said and hugged his mother. 'It's bath time, straight through.'

'Thanks, David,' his relieved father said as his mother disappeared into the kitchen.

'I hope she remembers whose child it is.'

'She will. I'll see to that.'

Lavinia Thomas paused in the doorway, the picture of her grandson in his bath was all she wanted. 'Celeste, I'm sorry for what I said. I hope we can be friends.'

A wary Celeste looked at her mother-in-law. David had told her all she needed to know. 'Of course, Mrs Thomas. Do you want to help bathe him?'

'I'd love to. Here, let me show you how to do that.'

'That's quite all right, Mrs Thomas. This is how my mother showed me.'

'Oh.'

David smiled at his father. 'You were saying, Dad?'

Douglas Blake stood to attention in front of Chief Constable George Carney's desk.

'I will tell you now, Blake, it is easy for me to promote a constable to sergeant. However, for you the changes and responsibilities are huge. You are now no longer a plain constable. And, although you work amongst them you are a supervisor. You have not only the role as a disciplinarian it is up to you to train them. And, let me stress that should you ever have to report any officer under your command the first thing I will examine is your role; could you have done something to prevent this from happening? Are you in any way culpable? Which is why you will be on probation for twelve months.

You have shown talent. A desire to do the task. And you have passed your inspector's examination. And who knows what the future holds. You will be transferred as detective sergeant to Hecton, Monday next.

This is not the end
Or the beginning of the end.
It is, however, the end of the beginning.

(Thanks to Winston Churchill)

If you enjoyed Dance With The Devil please tell your friends. If you didn't, please tell me.

The story continues in The Blooding of Brian Blake, Nemesis, Counting The Dead, Death in The Slushpile, Sylvester, Machello and Ægis

https://jonmasonbooks.com

Don't miss out!

Visit the website below and you can sign up to receive emails whenever Jon Mason publishes a new book. There's no charge and no obligation.

https://books2read.com/r/B-A-ZRTW-NWHKC

BOOKS 2 READ

Connecting independent readers to independent writers.

Did you love *Dance With the Devil*? Then you should read *The Blooding of Brian Blake*[1] by Jon Mason!

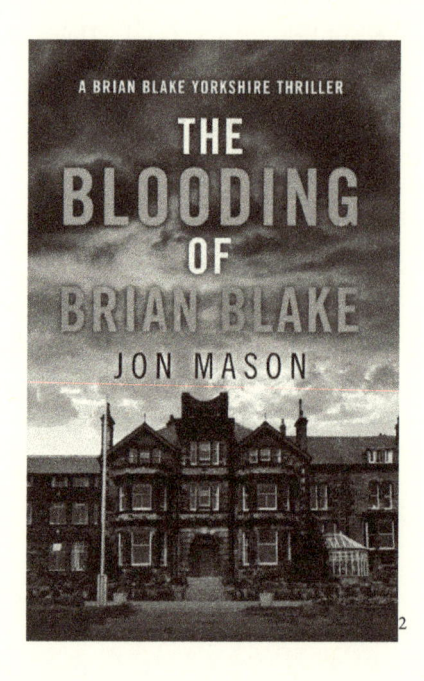

Fourteen years after the murder of his detective sergeant father, Brian Blake graduates from university and follows in his father's footsteps.

No3 District Police Training Centre, Pannal Ash, Harrogate. He knew the work would be hard. What he didn't anticipate was the aggression and violence from a small minority. The ramifications of an interview by MI5. Nor the maelstrom when confronted by a forgotten face from his past. A cold-blooded killer who would think nothing of killing anyone who stood in his way.

Read more at www.jonmasonbooks.com.

---

1. https://books2read.com/u/3yQLnZ
2. https://books2read.com/u/3yQLnZ

Also by Jon Mason

Blake Detective Series
Dance With the Devil
The Blooding of Brian Blake
Nemesis
Counting The Dead

Watch for more at www.jonmasonbooks.com.

About the Author

JON was born into post WW2 Yorkshire in England. His brother Stuart was born in 1938. His father, demobbed from the RAF where he had been a Dispatch Rider, returned to the tailoring industry. His mother had spent the war years x-raying wheels for battle tanks.

They lived in a small, inner two-bedroomed terrace house. There was no damp-proof course, double glazing, central heating or hot water on tap. The tin bath hung from a nail under the stairs and the lavatory was across the back yard..

Leaving school in 1962 he joined the West Riding Constabulary as a Cadet and as a Constable in 1965. His initial training carried out at No3 District Police Training Centre, Pannal Ash, Harrogate, in the then North Riding of Yorkshire.

Over the next three decades he gained experience across much of what the police service has to offer. 1965-70 on uniform beat patrol. From 1970-75 in the Road Traffic Division as an advanced driver and also where he was firearms trained. From 1975-77 Force Control where he learned his radio and computer skills before being promoted to the Western Area Control Room in January of 1977, Twelve months later he was seconded to the fledgling Computer Development Unit working with Ferranti International in the development of Stage 4 of a resource handling and incident recording system known as Command and Control (Not big Brother) and the setting up of the Communications Training Wing at the West Yorkshire Police training school. December 1983 saw him transferred to an inner city sub-division where he spent the last 10 years of his service as uniform patrol sergeant where he also worked closely with the Air Support Unit, Custody Officer and the last four years as the Station Sergeant.

In May of 1967 Jon and his fiancee married. A marriage which so far has lasted for over 56 years. They had two children, tragically Andrew, the elder, died of a heart attack in January 2018 - he was 48. Their daughter is still going strong.

Prior to retirement Jon qualified as a fitness instructor and subsequently head-hunted to work in a new community based cardiac rehab programme where he had the opportunity to study cardiology at Leeds University Medical School and exercise physiology at Carnegie. He also studied bio-mechanics.

All that knowledge and experience Jon brings to his books.

Read more at www.jonmasonbooks.com.

www.ingramcontent.com/pod-product-compliance
Ingram Content Group UK Ltd.
Pitfield, Milton Keynes, MK11 3LW, UK
UKHW041959260225
455621UK00001B/11